RANDALL
Randall, Rona,
Love and Dr Maynard

WITHDRAWN
12.14

LOVE AND DR MAYNARD

D0813896

Dodge City Public Library
Dodge City, Kansas

Dodge City Public Library

Dodge City Public Library
Dodge City, Kansas

LOVE AND DR MAYNARD

Rona Randall

Chivers Press
Bath, England   •   **Thorndike Press**
Waterville, Maine USA

This Large Print edition is published by Chivers Press, England, and by Thorndike Press, USA.

Published in 2002 in the U.K. by arrangement with the author c/o Juliet Burton Literary Agency.

Published in 2002 in the U.S. by arrangement with Juliet Burton Literary Agency.

U.K. Hardcover ISBN 0–7540–7434–X (Chivers Large Print)
U.K. Softcover ISBN 0–7540–7435–8 (Camden Large Print)
U.S. Softcover ISBN 0–7862–4538–7 (Nightingale Series Edition)

Copyright © Rona Randall, 1959

All rights reserved.

The text of this Large Print edition is unabridged.
Other aspects of the book may vary from the original edition.

Set in 16 pt. New Times Roman.

Printed in Great Britain on acid-free paper.

British Library Cataloguing in Publication Data available

Library of Congress Cataloging-in-Publication Data

Randall, Rona, 1911–
    Love and Dr. Maynard / Rona Randall.
       p. cm.
    ISBN 0–7862–4538–7 (lg. print : sc : alk. paper)
    1. Cornwall (England : County)—Fiction. 2. Physicians—Fiction.
    3. Large type books. I. Title: Love and Doctor Maynard. II. Title.
PR6035.A58 L68 2002
823'.912—dc21   2002075213

CHAPTER ONE

It was going to be a wrench, leaving the place—Christopher knew that. But it had to be faced. After all, he had come as old Doctor Peterson's assistant purely on a temporary basis. Six months, no more; six months in which his damaged leg could really recover, and his health with it. Funny, he thought, I imagined six months in the depths of Cornwall would be a life sentence; instead, they're too fleeting, too lovely to part with. And in a few weeks they'll be over and Sally Peterson will take my place.

What kind of a girl was she, this daughter of the old doctor? A blue-stocking, of course. Sure to be. Beefy and bespectacled, no doubt. Of course, not all women doctors were unattractive, but most of the really feminine ones married and gave up medicine, and the rest became dedicated to their work.

Interesting as they were medically, diverticulums and mastectomies were hardly the subjects for companionable conversation between a man and a woman. For his part, he preferred girls like Diana, who knew nothing of such things.

All he'd seen of Sally Peterson, so far, was a photograph upon her father's desk, and that taken a few years earlier. The face was shy and

1

unassuming; pleasant, in an unspectacular way; round, with the puppy fat of girlhood. But the old man adored her, of course. She was his only child.

But what had hospital life done to her? Taken away the soft lines of the mouth and replaced them with the calm, detached, resolute line he had seen so often on the faces of busy hospital doctors? They had streams of patients to see every day; tragedy stalked them. They had to steel themselves to face up to disappointment and heart-break and loss of hope. On the other hand, these were counterbalanced by success and faith and dogged determination.

Hospital staff were wonderful folk, as he well knew. He'd done his share of such work in the mining areas of Wales. That was how he had injured his leg and had been discharged from hospital duty. Going out on an ambulance call when a mine shaft had collapsed, he'd gone down with the rescue squad himself and sustained injuries as a result —not only to his leg, but internally due to escaping gases. Nothing chronic, but enough to make him useless in that particular job for six months or so. 'A quiet spell in the country is what you need,' they told him. 'You'll be as fit as a fiddle again, after that.'

So here he was, at Tresanton, and when he went, here his heart would remain.

Well, he had a few more weeks, so he'd be

2

wise to make the most of them. He'd sail in the creek with Diana and go fishing with old Simon from Porthscatho, but most of the time he'd be driving around the narrow country lanes, visiting the local people whom he had come to know and love. Old Mrs. Cruwys, with her arthritis, and Carl Penwyn, with his dicky heart, and Pete Trewin, who suffered from nothing more than Saturday night over-indulgence at The Rose and Crown. They'd accepted him, these people with strange-sounding names and nuances in their voices which suggested some remote foreign ancestry. They'd accepted him, and they liked him. He wanted to stay with them for ever.

But it wasn't possible. A bargain was a bargain and he had to stick to his side of it. 'When Sally's done her hospital tour of duty she'll become my assistant—I think you should know that at the outset, Maynard. It's always been my dream to have her beside me, ever since she began her medical training. And, of course, there's always been a Doctor Peterson in Tresanton. My father and his father before him—and a generation before that, also. Well, I hadn't a son, but Sally's been as good as one. She'll take my place, eventually.'

Perhaps it was that which had planted the picture in Christopher's mind—the picture of a masculine, striding young woman.

'And if she marries, sir?' (Not that he could imagine such a girl doing so.)

The old man had brushed that aside.

'She'll marry some local man, of course. In fact,' he chuckled, 'I could name him already. *That's* been taken for granted since they were children. But Martin is one of us. He won't mind her practising after they're married, I'm quite certain of that.'

Martin? he wondered. Martin Penfold, the solicitor's son? Chris had met him, and a thoroughly nice fellow he was. Diana loved teasing him—but then, she loved teasing anyone who didn't retaliate, and Martin Penfold was much too gentlemanly to exchange banter with the daughter of the great Joseph Langdon. He was a decent chap, of course—good looking, too—but, for some inexplicable reason, Chris's first encounter with Martin Penfold had been unimpressive.

So he'd changed the subject.

'You're proud of your daughter, aren't you, sir?'

'Proud? That's an inadequate word, my boy. Sally's my whole life.'

So Chris had accepted the post for six months. 'Mind you,' said old Doctor Peterson, 'until recently one doctor was quite sufficient for this village, but since Joseph Langdon developed the local china clay into a flourishing industry, the population has increased to such a degree that an old man can't cope. Besides, I haven't been too well lately, so I need you badly, and I hope you'll

4

stay until Sally takes over.'

And in six weeks she would, so time was fleeting and he had to make the most of it.

From the window of Doctor Peterson's study, where he was working, Christopher could see the winding hill out of Tresanton. Descending it was Diana's car—long and low and luxurious. His heart quickened at the sight of it, for it meant that she was coming to see him, even though she might make the excuse that she was merely dropping in on the old doctor. Diana's visits had become more frequent since Doctor Peterson took on a locum, a fact which the old man regarded with an indulgent eye.

Diana was extremely pretty, dressed exquisitely, and had a figure any model might envy. That he was more than a little in love with her, Christopher had already acknowledged—but only to himself.

There were barriers between them, and one in particular. She was Joseph Langdon's daughter and her father's wealth was a discouragement to a man who had as little as young Doctor Maynard. As yet, he was a mere locum, but his father had left him some money when he died, enough to buy a modest house, perhaps, but could a girl like Diana be expected to accept a modest house and all it entailed? The humdrum maintenance of it; the middle-class background?

Christopher thrust the thought aside. It was

enough, for now, to give himself up to the delight of her company, and when she whirled into the drive leading to the old house, the lovely, mellow old house in which the Petersons had lived for generations, he forgot everything but pleasure at the sight of her. Diana always gladdened the eye.

He went to meet her. She waved a friendly hand and linked a companionable arm in his.

'Sally arrived yet?' she asked.

'Not yet. Her father has gone to meet her at Truro.'

'Good. That means we're alone for five minutes.'

The pressure on his arm increased imperceptibly and she looked up at him with a glance which was at once both intimate and provocative.

'Glad to see me, Chris?'

'You know I am.'

'Then let's sit in the summer-house and you can tell me just how much.'

She was enchanting. He laughed down at her and obeyed, but in the shelter of the arbour she glanced at him carefully and said:

'You're preoccupied, Chris. What about?'

'Many things. My departure, in particular.'

'Your departure! But you're not going yet?'

'Not for six weeks—but six weeks can fly.'

She dropped her head against his shoulder. 'You don't want to go, do you, Chris?' she asked in a low voice.

'No, I don't.'

'Why?'

'Many reasons. I like the work, the place, the people. I feel at home here. In six months a doctor begins to know his patients; they begin to matter to him. I thought, when I came, that it would be merely a marking-time; a preliminary to better things. 'Fill your lungs with good fresh air,' they said, 'and you'll be fit for anything.' So I had plans to get a job in London after that.'

'And now?'

'Now I want to stay right here, in Tresanton.'

She looked up at him. Her charming face was very close to his own.

'Aren't *I* included in your reasons for staying?'

'You know you are,' he answered gruffly, 'but I'm not in a position to tell you so.'

'I don't see why not.' She laughed a little, kissed him lightly upon the cheek, and said:

'Darling, don't look so worried—I've an idea; a solution. Why shouldn't you get a job in Falmouth or Truro? Then we'd be near each other still.'

'Because the only jobs in Falmouth or Truro would be hospital jobs and I've done my share of foot-slogging on the wards. I like the personal touch of a G.P.'s life. I like to know my patients as people, as neighbours. I get a kick out of being greeted as I drive through the

7

village and hearing people call me by name, instead of being known as 'that bloke in Out-Patients."'

'Then why not start a practice of your own here?'

'My dear, there are such things as Executive Councils and Regional Boards to contend with nowadays. A doctor can't just stick up a plate by his door. He has to be vetted and passed and permitted and all the rest of it. Anyway, Tresanton only really needs one doctor, even though the population *has* increased. It was a hamlet before; now it's an outsize village—rapidly expanding, I admit, but still not big enough to justify two G.P.s and personally I hope it never does grow to such a size. If George Peterson were not a sick man—and he is—he'd be able to cope well enough alone, and with his daughter to help him another doctor would certainly be superfluous.'

'What *is* the matter with Doctor P. ?'

'His heart isn't all it should be.'

'Poor pet. Does Sally know?'

'Yes. He told me he'd been quite frank with her about it last time she came home.'

'Then poor Sally, too—she adores him.'

'He'll probably last for years yet—I hope he does. He's one of the finest men I've ever known.'

'Everyone in Tresanton loves him. It's a pity they don't feel the same way about *my* father.'

'They admire him very much.'

8

'That isn't the same thing at all, and you know it.' She changed the subject abruptly. 'So you'll be going, after all. Do you know, I didn't really believe you would? I felt all along that something would intervene; something would happen to keep you here.'

'Well,' said Chris glumly, 'it won't.'

'I refuse to give up hope! Life always turns out the way I want it—why should it refuse to now?'

He had to laugh. Her bland optimism, her certainty that life would never defraud her, awakened an amused tenderness within him.

'What is Sally like?' he asked. '*Really* like, I mean?'

Diana looked surprised.

'You've met her, surely?'

'No. On the two occasions she's had leave since I came, I've been on leave, too.'

'Visiting your Aunt Helen,' Diana said dryly. 'I remember.'

She remembered because, on each occasion, she had wanted him to partner her to some social event, but Christopher's sense of duty to the aunt who had brought him up was unswerving. Privately, Diana considered it a little tiresome—but sweet, of course. Fidelity was a desirable quality in a man, but, taken to extremes, mightn't it be a little cloying?

'Yes, I do remember,' she repeated. 'Doctor Peterson gave you the weekend off each time, because Sally would be here to help him. How

9

funny to think that you have never met!'

'What is she like?' he asked again. He was naturally curious about this girl who, in so short a time, would be his successor.

Diana shrugged.

'Difficult to describe, really. I've known her nearly all my life and to me—well—she's just Sally. Nice and reliable and rather homely—like antimacassars and muffins for tea.'

'Stodgy, in fact.'

'Well—ordinary, I must admit. But perhaps London has spruced her up a bit. I haven't seen her myself since she took this hospital job. I can't imagine the East End having a brightening effect, though, can you?'

'Does she need brightening?'

'Not exactly. Just smartening up a bit. Where dress was concerned, she never had a clue.' Diana brushed an invisible speck of dust from her own immaculate linen suit—the simplicity of which disguised its elaborate price.

To his own surprise, Christopher said:

'Perhaps she couldn't afford much in the way of clothes.'

'There I agree. Doctor Peterson's as poor as a church mouse—everyone one knows that. He values family traditions too much—this house, for instance.' Her glance ran over the mellow bricks with unstinted admiration. 'Of course, it's lovely and I don't blame him, but until Daddy's clay works flourished and brought more workers to the district goodness knows how the Petersons managed to cling to this place!'

'It's worth clinging to, all the same.'

'There I agree again. I love Creek House myself. It's unpretentious, but absolutely full of character and quite beautiful—but where was I? Oh, yes—Sally. She's all right. You'll like her, I'm sure. Everyone does.'

'Including you?'

'Of course. I'm her greatest friend.'

That surprised him. Somehow, he couldn't imagine Diana being intimate friends with a blue-stocking—or a dowd.

'We went to school together,' she explained. 'Kindergarten, then High School. Sally won a scholarship, but I . . .' She shrugged and smiled with deprecating charm. 'Can you imagine *me* winning scholarships, or even trying to? Luckily, I didn't have to. Daddy's always been content for me to be a lily of the field.'

And a very lovely one, he thought.

'Then, of course, I went off to St. Germaine's . . .'

He knew all about that—the finishing school in Paris, the polishing of the shell, the perfecting of the product which Joseph Langdon was determined to make of his daughter. Anything less than perfection would have been a betrayal of his own success.

'And when I came back, Sally was already a medical student—another scholarship, of

11

course.'

'She must have been clever.'

'I always thought so, but *she* declared that she had to study more than the rest of us, for her father's sake—to keep up the family tradition, I suppose. In fact, she was so industrious that she made me feel uncomfortable.'

'And yet you remained friends?'

'Of course. We're fond of one another. The ties of childhood, I expect, although, really, we're quite different. And she's a sweet thing, although so earnest. Earnest about everything. "I've *got* to win that scholarship," she'd say, and go home and swot when everyone else was enjoying themselves. Between you and me, darling, I found it a little difficult to live up to.'

So the blue-stocking part was right, he thought.

He had a picture of Sally Peterson now firmly in his mind; a picture of an industrious woman doctor serving the community well. Would she actually marry Martin Penfold? Why not? The fellow would become her counterpart—the earnest local solicitor emulating his wife's industrious example.

Christopher rose abruptly and stood outside the summerhouse, frowning at the gravel path beneath his feet. He kicked a pebble savagely. Didn't he want Tresanton to be served by such a doctor? Of course, he did! But he wanted to be that doctor himself.

There was the sound of an approaching engine and George Peterson's ancient car turned in at the gate.

'Here they come!' Diana said lightly and, with her hand in his, Christopher went to meet them.

CHAPTER TWO

And it was thus that Sally Peterson first saw him—walking towards her across the lawn of Creek House, with Diana's hand in his. There was an intimacy about the gesture which struck her at once, and then she forgot about it in that, swift first impression of the man himself. The impression of strength and rugged determination and virility.

'An able young doctor,' her father had called Chris Maynard. An understatement! Sally thought with secret humour. He was a man of invincible character and she wouldn't like to make an enemy of him.

Not that she was likely to. She'd take his place in a few weeks' time and then he'd go right out of her life. As for this brief weekend—well, there would scarcely be time to get acquainted. Especially if that possessive hand of Diana's maintained its hold upon him . . .

Once a man yielded to Diana (and didn't

they all?) he became oblivious of any other girl.

And then Sally was stepping out of the car and her father was making introductions and Christopher Maynard was looking down at her with obvious surprise. But why? What did he expect? she wondered.

She detached her hand from his strong clasp, aware of a swift and unaccountable reaction. In an indefinable way this man disturbed her and because she couldn't explain it, she was annoyed by it.

'Sally, darling! How wonderful to see you!'

Diana's cool cheek was against her own— lovely Diana, exquisite as ever. And then she was holding Sally at arm's length and viewing her with affectionate eyes. 'My, my!' she said. 'The past two years have knocked some weight off you!'

Sally laughed.

'It's all that exercise at the hospital. A house-physician doesn't get much time to sit down!'

Her father placed a fond arm about her shoulders—an increasingly fragile arm, Sally noticed in concern. If the past two years had slimmed her, they had done more than that to her father. Every time she came home he seemed a little more shrunken than before; a little more aged.

'Well,' he declared, 'Martha will fatten her up as soon as she's home for good. Meanwhile,

14

we'll see what can be done this weekend—eh, my dear? If you don't eat Martha's abundant meals, there'll be trouble, Sally.'

'I can vouch for that,' Christopher laughed. 'In the few months I've been here she's practically doubled my weight.'

'Is that why you're such an ardent athlete, darling—to keep it under control?' Diana put in. The 'darling' didn't escape Sally—not that it meant anything, of course. In the easy social world in which Diana moved endearments were bandied about unthinkingly.

They moved towards the house. Diana said:

'I must be off. I just dropped in to see if Sally had arrived and to tell you that we expect you all for dinner tonight. Will eight o'clock suit you?'

Mutual alarm sprang between Sally and her father. Their evenings together now were so rare, so precious, that to be compelled to share one with outsiders—especially her first night home—was the last thing they desired.

Besides, the weekend would be so fleeting— from Friday until Tuesday morning, no more; three precious days which she had planned to spend with her father as much as possible.

They might go fishing in the creek, or sail out of Porthscatho after mackerel; they might merely sit in the garden and talk of the future—the future for which they had both worked and planned and which was now so close at hand. Or they might stay in the long, cool drawing-room, reading and talking desultorily, until it was time to go to bed.

A dozen things they might do, but together, alone, shared with no one else.

No one? Sally thought with a jerk. There was this young Doctor Maynard who would, at least, dine with them. Since coming to Tresanton as her father's locum he had lived at Creek House—a convenient arrangement all round. The place was plenty big enough and he had his own sitting-room at the back of the house to which, she hoped, he would retire after dinner.

But now they were being whisked off to Diana's splendid home. They'd have to dress up and be socially-minded when all they wanted, she and her father, was to be together in the mellow loveliness of their own home.

Besides, it would all be so overwhelming at The Towers. Diana's home had none of the simplicity of her own, nor would the meal be on Martha's simple lines, but lavish and wonderful, and afterwards her father would complain fretfully about his indigestion ...

Sally checked a smile. No one saw it but Christopher Maynard, who was still studying her in some surprise. In fact, he couldn't take his eyes from her—not because she was particularly pretty or particularly impressive, but because she was so totally different from his expectations.

Different, too, from Diana's portrait.

16

He saw that betraying flicker of amusement beside her mouth—the mouth so little changed from the young and gentle one of the photograph—and wondered what fleeting thought provoked it. Far from being the stolid young woman of his imagination, she was slim and young, with humour in her face—character, too, plenty of that, but not the aggressive sort, the dictatorial sort. She had short dark hair, neatly cut, and although her features were unspectacular they were attractive. She wore a suit in a pleasant shade of blue, and looked well in it. She was not over-sophisticated, but well-dressed and quietly assured. Altogether, she was an agreeable surprise.

All this he observed in their brief encounter, then jerked to awareness—to hear Diana saying:

'Father will be delighted to see you again, Sally. We'll expect you at eight, then?'

Sally Peterson's answer appeared to be startling—Christopher didn't know why. He saw Diana stand stock still in her tracks and stare back at the girl as if she hadn't heard all right.

'Any other night—but not tonight,' Sally said. 'I'm sorry, Diana, but I want to dine at home with Father.'

There didn't seem anything particularly offensive about that. It was said quite pleasantly and reasonably. 'I'm sure you understand,' Sally went on. 'As Junior House-

17

Physician I haven't been able to come and go as I choose; my weekends at home have become very precious.'

Diana's slim shoulders shrugged; her thin eyebrows raised. 'Please yourself,' she said indifferently, and turned towards the car. Old Doctor Peterson hastily opened the door for her.

'Give my kind regards to Joseph . . .' he began, but Diana cut across his words.

'He'll be furious. You know that, don't you, Doctor P. ?'

'Because I send my good wishes?' the old man queried gently.

'Of course not. Because you refuse to dine with us.'

Sally said clearly:

'Nonsense, Diana. We just ask for tonight at home, that's all. Is it so unreasonable?'

Diana gave her a long, level glance. Something had happened to Sally in the last two years, she thought. She'd become—independent. That was it—independent. Not afraid to speak up for herself. Different from the old days, when she'd been Diana's devoted little shadow . . .

'Please yourselves—but *you'll* come, at any rate, won't you, Christopher?'

'I'd be delighted,' he answered—partly because it was the truth, and partly because he thought it might be tactful to let the old Doctor and his daughter have a *tête-à-tête*

18

evening.

'Good.' Diana's long hand covered his own as it lay upon the door of her car. There was a caress in her touch and it sent a warm fire through his veins, but he was a little embarrassed and was glad, on turning round, to see that Sally and her father were not watching.

''Till eight then—or a little before, if you can make it,' Diana said.

'I'll take surgery tonight, so that he may,' George Peterson put in.

'You'll do nothing of the sort, sir. It's my duty turn and I'm not foisting it on to you.'

'You won't be late?' Diana said anxiously.

'Not unless an unexpected case comes in, and I don't anticipate that. We know the state of health of most Tresanton inhabitants,' he answered with a smile.

'Well, have any calls put through to The Towers, darling—although I'll be furious if anything spoils our evening!'

With a wave, a smile, and a roar of a powerful engine, she was gone.

Sally went into the house. Within the wide, dim hall she stood still and glanced about her.

'It's good to be back, Father. So terribly good!'

'And soon it will be for always,' he answered affectionately. 'I'm looking forward to having you work beside me, my dear. That has always been my dream.'

'I know.'

Wasn't that why she had worked and studied until she'd felt she could drop? Wasn't that why she had denied herself the pleasures and the fun most girls of her age had taken for granted? There had always been a Doctor Peterson in Tresanton—that was the tradition which meant so much to her father; indeed, to herself as well. But in achieving it she had had to forgo much. Dances had been few in her life; boy friends nil. Except Martin, of course—he was always there. Stolid and reliable and faithful. Dear Martin, she thought affectionately. What would I have done without him?

But she'd managed well enough in London. There had been doctors at the hospital who had paid attention to her—taken her out to dine; to theatres; even to occasional parties. She had never lacked partners at hospital dances. And so, gradually, she had come out of her shell, begun to take an interest in clothes, in her appearance, lost her shyness and self-consciousness, until, in the end, she was the most popular young doctor on the wards. They'd be sorry to see her go, at St. Mark's. She'd be sorry, too, but to return to Tresanton as young Doctor Peterson, the fourth generation, had been her aim, her goal, and, as he said, her father's dream.

There was a deep affection between these two—all the deeper, perhaps, because she had been motherless at an early age and so they had lived together alone, until her medical-student days—alone but for old Martha, who had been more than housekeeper to them. She had taken the place of Sally's mother and practically brought her up, so she was one of the family—a close-knit little family, devoted to one another.

Sally was glad to observe that young Doctor Maynard had left them alone. He was sitting outside on the terrace, reading a newspaper. Sally studied the back of his head and observed that it was well-shaped; that his shoulders were broad and, she suspected, very muscular. Her father followed her glance and nodded approvingly.

'A nice fellow, Maynard. Good doctor, too. The patients like him.'

'*And* Diana?'

George Peterson's eyes twinkled.

'You noticed that, did you? They see a lot of each other, it's true, but whether Joseph Langdon would accept him as a son-in-law is another matter.'

Sally said swiftly:

'Does he want to be Joseph Langdon's son-in-law?'

Her father turned a bland glance upon her.

'My child, I have no idea. But in any case, I should think the question would be whether *Diana* wants him for the position—and what Diana wants, she usually gets.'

21

Sally knew that well enough. Not that Diana could be blamed entirely for her assumption that life should pour everything into her lap. Her father had been doing that from the day she was born, so how could she be expected to contemplate denial?

Sally said:

'Well, if they do marry, I hope they'll be very happy.' And she meant it.

'As to that, my dear, I don't even know if the question has arisen,' George Peterson answered mildly. 'Because they see a lot of each other doesn't necessarily mean that they're in love.'

No, thought Sally, it doesn't. And felt a swift and illogical relief.

CHAPTER THREE

When Sally came downstairs for dinner that night she found young Doctor Maynard alone in the drawing-room.

'Father not down yet?' she asked pleasantly.

Chris rose swiftly.

'Not yet. May I get you a drink?'

'Sherry, please. Medium.'

She observed his hands as he lifted the decanter—the well-shaped strong hands which Diana had covered so possessively with her own. It wasn't my imagination, either, Sally thought. That touch of Diana's had been more than a light flirtatious gesture. And he hadn't drawn away . . .

'I'm glad we're alone, Doctor. I wanted to have a word with you about my father.'

He answered carefully:

'What about your father?'

She took the glass he extended, but paused before drinking.

'Is he worse? Tell me frankly—you're with him every day. You should know.'

'I only know that he works too hard; that he should ease up a little.'

'And he won't, of course. That doesn't surprise me. His work is his life.'

'No,' Christopher answered gently. '*You* are his life.'

Her widely-spaced eyes looked up at him and he saw that they were a deep and lovely grey; the sort of grey which reflected whatever colour she was wearing. This afternoon it had been blue. Now it was green—chartreuse green. Not a model dress by any means, but very charming. Or the figure that wore it was charming—he wasn't sure which and didn't like to stare too hard to find out.

'If it comes to that, Doctor Maynard, *he* is mine.'

He was touched by the simplicity of the statement, just as he had been touched when he first saw them together, father and daughter. They loved one another deeply and simply; their attitude to each other was quiet and companionable, without any maudlin sentiment, but there was no mistaking the strength of their devotion.

'But you have all your life before you . . .' he began.

'And Father? How much has he?'

'The specialists say an unspecified period, so long as he takes care.'

'And does he take care? Tell me,' she asked anxiously. 'I am not here to keep an eye on him, you know, and Martha has never been able to rule him.'

'Can anyone rule a man as devoted to medicine as your father?'

She smiled. 'No. But I wish he'd apply that diligence to himself. He looks tired, Doctor Maynard—more tired than when I last came home.'

'Are you wondering whether he puts in too many working hours? Believe me, I try to relieve him of as many as possible.'

'I know you do. He has told me so. In fact, he has told me a lot about you—particularly this time. When I came home before he merely said how satisfied he was with you, but now it is obvious that he has become pretty dependent upon you.'

'And will be upon you, when you take my place.'

'Yes. We've waited so long for our partnership to materialise—we've dreamed of it for years.'

'I'm sure you'll run the practice well. I know how well qualified you are and, of course, the people here know you.'

'I hope they do more than that,' she answered quietly. 'I hope they love me as much as they do my father—and as much as I do them.'

He was aware of a swift response, an understanding born of his own feeling for Tresanton and its people. If I can feel like this in less than six months, he thought, how must she feel, after a lifetime? *One* of them, of course. *Belonging.*

He raised his glass.

'Here's to your return,' he said. 'To the fulfilment of all your hopes and dreams—your father's too.'

'Thank you,' she answered simply. She was rather touched. If, as her father suggested, Christopher Maynard had settled down here well and happily, he could be justified in being a little less generous in his good wishes for her return. Especially if her return meant him leaving the district—and Diana.

There was Diana back again, like an intervening barrier. The thought startled Sally. It was nothing to her if this man was attracted to Diana. All men were. She had watched it happen since her early teens.

'You've been happy here, Doctor?' she asked.

He turned away, answering abruptly: 'Very happy, thank you.' That was all he could trust himself to say.

There was a sudden silence between them. A moment ago they had felt at ease—even united in an understanding which could only be nameless; a sort of awareness of one another which neither could pin down or define. Now they were strangers again.

She noticed that he was wearing a dinner jacket—the correct attire, of course, for a guest at The Towers, but at Creek House her father could wear his comfortable old bedroom slippers and she, if she wished, could change into a housecoat and relax. She was more than ever thankful that she had side-stepped Diana's invitation for dinner tonight.

Conversation seemed to have died between them; the atmosphere became strained. She began to wish that her father would come down and Christopher glanced at his watch, as if seeking escape. He didn't know why he should feel self-conscious in the presence of this girl. He wasn't attracted to her, although she was a pleasant surprise after the picture he had built up in his mind—but, all the same, he *was* aware of her.

Was she summing him up, secretly, in her mind? Was she studying his averted back and thinking: When he leaves Tresanton no one will miss him—he was only temporary; a make-shift; a stop-gap? He told himself not to be a

26

fool. What did it matter to him what this girl was thinking?

He turned, and saw that she was looking out of a window on to the shadowy garden. 'I love this place,' she said quietly, and he realised that she wasn't thinking about him at all. She had completely forgotten him, in fact, and was merely musing aloud.

'It's a lovely garden,' he agreed. 'A lovely house.'

She turned to him with a rare and brilliant smile—a smile so happy that her serious young face was transformed.

'You like it, too, Doctor? I'm glad.'

'Everyone calls me Chris,' he answered. 'Including your father.'

'Chris, then. And I'm glad you like Creek House.'

'Who could fail to? Even Diana loves it.'

She looked surprised.

'I didn't know that. I should have thought that, compared with The Towers, it might seem—well—unattractive.'

'This house is a home,' he answered simply.

He didn't mean to disparage Joseph Langdon's magnificent residence—he was merely stating what he felt. Sometimes he suspected that Diana felt it, too; that she would have preferred a home like Sally's, but was too loyal to her father to say so. That was one of the things he liked about Diana. Liked? Well—loved, perhaps. He wasn't really sure about that, yet. Earlier today he thought he was, but now, for some quite nameless reason, doubt had crept in.

Nevertheless, he was looking forward to his evening with her—even in her father's overbearing presence. This expectation was intensified when he saw Martin Penfold's car turning in at the gates of Creek House and the calm, regular features of the man sitting at the wheel.

Sally heard the car, too, and rose. She hoped it wasn't a visitor—no one who should be asked to dine. A patient, perhaps. An unexpected call which Doctor Maynard could take. She crossed to the window which overlooked the drive and recognised Martin's neat saloon car. Her face lightened immediately and she ran to the door to meet him.

Christopher laid down his glass. This, he thought, is my cue to depart. He didn't want to be present at the reunion of these two; not if, as her father suggested, the man was Sally's potential husband. So he walked out into the hall and arrived just in time to see Martin standing in the open doorway, holding both of Sally's hands in his.

They kissed each other affectionately. It wasn't a passionate kiss, nor the kiss of lovers reunited, but it was sufficient to make Christopher Maynard—quite illogically—want to thrust the man aside.

Martin Penfold linked his arm in Sally's and

28

turned with her towards the drawing-room, and neither of them heard Christopher take his departure.

'Let me look at you,' Martin said, the minute the door closed. He held her at arm's length, surveying her fondly, then a slight frown touched his handsome brow.

'You've lost weight, Sally.'

'I've no complaints about that!'

'Well, I have. I don't like it. You've been working too hard—and eating insufficiently.'

'On the contrary, I eat like a horse! Believe me, when you've done a stretch on Out-Patients and then a round of the wards, and *then* an emergency delivery because no one else was available at that particular moment, a coffee-and-sandwich doesn't satisfy the appetite!' She laughed and gave him a friendly shake. 'Dear Martin, you're always so concerned about me—quite needlessly!'

'Of course, I'm concerned about you. I love you—you know that.'

Her laughter died. She was fond of Martin, terribly fond, but she wasn't ready for love yet—not real love; serious love; the settle-down-together kind. There was too much to do; too much on her programme.

His arms went about her suddenly. His cheek pressed against her hair. 'Marry me, Sally . . . marry me . . .'

She stood quite still. He sensed a reluctance in her stillness and glanced down at her. 'Why

29

do you hesitate?' he asked. 'You know it's always been taken for granted between us!'

She wanted to ask: By whom? but knew the answer. By him. By his parents. By her father. By everyone.

'Sally, why do you hesitate?' he asked again.

'Because I'm not *sure*, Martin.'

'Not sure—or just not ready?' His smile was gentle and understanding and she thought: Why was I afraid of hurting him? He isn't hurt at all. He isn't hurt because *he* is sure and so he doesn't believe that anything could go wrong.

She drew away from him.

'I suppose that's the truth of it—I'm just not ready.' She threw out her hands in an expressive gesture—a pleading gesture. 'Don't you *see*, Martin? I have so much to do! So much to fulfil!'

'Such as?'

'Coming home to work with Father, for one thing. Being a doctor, for another. I want to be a *good* doctor, Martin—in fact, they tell me at St. Mark's that I am. Yes, that was from the super. himself! He told me they'd be sorry to see me go when my tour of duty ended.'

'That I can understand. Everyone at Tresanton was sorry to see you go to London. We love you, Sally. *I* love you.'

She put her hands upon his shoulders and looked up at him, her heart warm with affection.

30

'I know, Martin—I know. But try to understand this, too—that word of praise from the super. wasn't prompted by any prejudiced affection!' She laughed at the thought. 'No, it was utterly impartial—coldly clinical, if you like.'

'Nice of him.'

Her hands dropped from his shoulders. A wry touch of humour curved her mouth—the same amused little smile which Christopher had noticed that afternoon.

'He wasn't being "nice," Martin—he was offering me a job. He wanted me to stay at St. Mark's, on the permanent staff.'

'You refused, of course.'

The natural assumption vaguely annoyed her.

'Yes, I refused—but not because I wasn't tempted, or flattered, but because I wanted to come home to Tresanton to be the fourth Doctor Peterson. To carry on the tradition.'

'Now look here, Sally, that's all very well, but every Doctor Peterson so far has been a man.'

'And the next will be a woman. What's the difference?'

'Plenty. Women get married and have children . . .'

'And still carry on as doctors. Any objections?'

A smile of gratification spread across Martin's good-looking face.

31

'None at all—if that's an acceptance.'

'Not yet! Not yet!' she cried.

'Sally, please be sensible! You don't *have* to carry on your family's tradition! You could chuck medicine and be my wife. Your father won't be retiring for ages yet, and when he does, this Doctor Maynard can take his place. I hear he's a good doctor, and he's certainly been accepted in these parts—unusual for a stranger, you must admit. They're not usually welcomed with open arms, but the villagers like him tremendously.'

She felt a pang of plain, honest-to-goodness jealousy. 'Do they, indeed? Well—I believe they like me, too, and will welcome me home just as my father will. Chris came on a temporary basis, after all.'

'Chris?' he echoed swiftly. 'I didn't know you were on Christian name terms . . .'

Martin could be unreasonably jealous, Sally knew. Sometimes, in the past, when Diana was getting all the attention and she very little, Sally had found Martin's jealousy a comforting and even flattering quality, but now she was merely annoyed.

'Everyone calls him Chris,' she said a trifle shortly. 'Why not?'

The sight of Martin's frowning young face softened her heart. She took hold of his hands and drew him down on to a couch.

'Listen, Martin. Ever since I began my medical training—even before, in fact—Father dreamed of my becoming his assistant here. He's pictured me working with him, learning from him, sharing his work and interests. You know how close we are to each other—particularly close, perhaps, because Mother died when I was a baby and we've been alone together ever since . . .'

'Your father should have married again.'

'Well, he didn't. He always said that no one could take Mother's place, in his life or mine, so perhaps we're more than averagely close in understanding. Even as a child I knew he dreamed of my becoming a doctor—he always advocated medicine as a career for women.'

'I don't know that I do,' Martin said a trifle glumly.

She gave him a friendly shake, then, seeing his look of despondency, she finished gently:

'One thing I *do* know, Martin—if I marry anyone at all there is no one I should like to marry more than you.'

He brightened visibly.

'So there's no one else in your life? No other man? No doctor in London? No one at all?'

She laughed spontaneously.

'No one at all, Martin, I can promise you that!

She meant it, too. And yet, inexplicably, felt that she was lying.

CHAPTER FOUR

Climbing the hill from the village, Chris could see the impressive outlines of Joseph Langdon's house—a turreted mansion he had built some years ago and of which he was inordinately proud. Chris sometimes had the unkind suspicion that it was meant to be an advertisement for the man's success and, in that, it certainly succeeded. Known to the local inhabitants as 'Langdon Palace,' it testified only too well to the man's abounding wealth.

Diana met Christopher in the wide, pillared hall—the hall which always reminded him of a Hollywood film set. To the right, a curving marble staircase swept upwards; to the left, a series of tall, ornate doors opened into luxurious rooms. He felt uncomfortable in this place—like an actor who couldn't play the part required of him.

And yet, when Diana appeared—running down the marble staircase in a cloud of flimsy georgette—all his discomfort vanished in the sheer pleasure of being with her. Her dress was ballet-length, full-skirted, emphasising skilfully her slender waist and pretty shoulders.

One of the things he admired most about Diana was her lack of conceit; she was aware of her beauty—how could she fail to be?—but never exploited it, never traded upon it, never made a man feel that he must constantly express his admiration. She accepted it as she accepted the luxurious background of this house—as part of her birthright. And yet she didn't over-value such things—indeed, he knew that she would be happier in a place like Creek House than at The Towers.

'Father's Folly' she had once derided it—gently, of course. But that had intimated to Chris precisely what he already guessed—that at heart Diana loved simple things.

She reached up and kissed him lightly upon the cheek—a gesture which could be exchanged between friends; fond friends. A non-committal gesture, signifying nothing. Nothing intimate or binding—or even promising, for that matter. She had the ability to keep him guessing always.

'Father's in a mood,' she warned. 'I'm counting on you to coax him out of it!'

The prospect wasn't too pleasing. Chris was only too well aware of how Joseph Langdon regarded him—as an impecunious young doctor aspiring for the hand of his daughter.

'I'm hardly the one to soothe his mood, my dear. Anyway, what provoked it?'

'The Royal Command was disobeyed,' she answered lightly. 'In other words, the two Doctor Petersons declined his summons . . .'

It seemed strange to talk of the 'two Doctor Petersons'—strange to think of that slip of a girl as a doctor at all. Sally—that was what he called her in his mind, because that was how

35

her father referred to her. But, of course, Christopher reminded himself she was fully qualified medically—well qualified, too.

'She isn't a bit as I imagined her,' Chris said meditatively.

Diana looked at him sharply.

'Who isn't?'

'Sally. She's taken me completely by surprise. I expected someone very earnest and tense . . .'

'She is earnest. I told you.'

'Yes—but in a different way.' He made a dissatisfied gesture. 'That isn't what I mean.'

'What do you mean?' Diana asked sweetly. 'That she's little and feminine and rather sweet?'

'Yes—that is just what I do mean.'

'And you'd expected someone masculine and striding and strong?'

'In a way. Certainly not a bit like this girl . . .'

'Sally's a pet—I told you that, too.'

He didn't remember those exact words, but he did remember, of course, that they'd been lifelong friends. Now it didn't seem so surprising. But the girl wasn't a dowd—in that, Diana had been wrong.

He said nothing, however, and turned with her towards the drawing-room. He could see Joseph Langdon's burly figure blocking the fireplace, a glass in one hand, the other thrust behind his back like Napoleon. He was a bulldog of a man, and proud of it.

36

'Ha—Maynard!' he barked. Only people of importance received a more amiable greeting. Chris smiled inwardly and held out his hand, so that Joseph Langdon had no choice but to shake it. The small, shrewd eyes, set like currants in a pudding of a face, surveyed him keenly. *Village doctor. Country G.P. As if my girl couldn't do better than that for herself.* Christopher could almost hear the thought, as if whispered into his ears through a microphone.

Diana's graceful hand held out a glass to Christopher. 'Dry Martini—mixed just as you like it,' she said.

The atmosphere in the room was tense—like the prelude to a storm. Suddenly it came.

'So that senile old doctor and his daughter decline to dine with me, eh? But *you* don't, young man. Why, I wonder?'

Despite the anger which darted through his brain, Chris answered calmly:

'Because it gives me pleasure to come, sir, and because I appreciated Doctor Peterson's desire to be alone with his daughter on her first evening home—the first evening of a brief weekend, and therefore doubly precious to them.'

'And you felt you ought to get out of the way—was that it? So an invitation to dine at The Towers came in useful.'

'I meant nothing of the sort, sir, and you know it. It was kind of you to invite me, I am

37

delighted to come, but I am also pleased to be able to leave the Petersons to dine together, alone.'

'Well, that's honest, at least.'

The truculent voice revealed a grudging admiration, but Christopher had not finished yet. Anger still pricked his mind like sand against the skin.

'Incidentally,' he added, 'Doctor Peterson is far from senile.'

'You've said the wrong thing, Father,' Diana put in sweetly. 'Chris is devote to Doctor P. So is the rest of Tresanton.'

Joseph Langdon waved a pudgy hand.

'A mere figure of speech. The fella's getting on—got to admit it. That's why he employed you, Maynard, and you know it.'

'He employed me because he simply isn't strong enough to carry on alone—not because he is too old, mentally or physically. The practice needs someone active and strong.'

'Thanks to *me*, I'd like to point out! Before I brought prosperity to this one-eyed little place, George Peterson had no more than a score of patients on his books. Now look at the population! And what's been responsible for the increase?'

'*Your* industry, *your* enterprise, *your* force and drive!' Diana chanted mechanically.

'Precisely. When I came here, twenty-odd years ago, no one had even thought of quarrying the local clay—and the finest white

38

china clay in the country, too. It took *me*—a rough northerner, I admit—to see the possibilities, and to exploit them. As a result, the population more than trebled—and old Doc. Peterson's practice, too. So who is *he* to turn his nose up at an invitation to The Towers?'

What was the use? Chris thought helplessly. Joseph Langdon was so sensitive to snub that he was for ever on the alert for one.

'I might also add,' the man continued truculently, 'that if it hadn't been for me that old house would have fallen down about his neck long ago. Only the sudden increase in his practice enabled him to save it—although, personally, I don't know why he wanted to. Must be a damp old house, standing down there beside the creek. Can't think why people admire it.'

I'm sure you can't, Diana thought bitterly, but then, poor poppet, anything that doesn't glitter can't possibly be gold, to you.

She loved her father—in many ways they were very alike—but she was impatient with him, and a little ashamed. His values were wrong—all wrong. She had acquired others, and it wasn't simply due to the expensive education he had given her.

Diana knew just what she wanted from life. The comforts and luxuries her father provided she took for granted—she would always have those, for his success assured them. But there

39

was one thing her father's money could never provide, and that was the right background—a background as unlike The Towers as it was possible to imagine. A background with roots and traditions.

Diana saw Creek House as the emblem of all she would like to be—something that belonged; that was revered, respected, loved.

Sally belonged to Tresanton as she herself could never belong, for Sally's roots were here, her family had lived here for generations—but no matter how long her own father lived in these parts and no matter how generously he donated to local charities, entertained the right people, or made public speeches, Diana knew that he would never be accepted in the way she longed for.

Yet Christopher had been. He'd fitted in from the start. Perhaps people felt at ease with him because he was unaffected and sincere. Her father's wealth intimidated them; his patronage insulted.

But with Christopher, she thought pathetically, *I* might be accepted, too . . .

Joseph Langdon suddenly decided to forgive Doctor Peterson's lapse from grace and said magnificently:

'Ah well, I can understand a man's desire to share an evening with his daughter. I've one of my own and I know how I'd feel if she left me for long. Those months at finishing school in Paris were pretty lonely for me, I can tell you.'

40

He glanced fondly at his daughter, and Chris felt a sudden pity for him. The great, the rich, or the successful, could sometimes find themselves bereft.

During dinner Joseph said abruptly:

'So Sally's back, eh?'

'For the weekend,' Diana told him.

'And when does she return for good?'

'In a few weeks,' Chris said.

'And you—what will you do then, young fella?'

'Look for a job in London, I think. That was what I planned.'

Approval came into Joseph Langdon's eyes.

'London? That's right, m'boy—aim high. Harley Street, eh—that where you plan to finish up?'

If so, said the silent implication, I might allow you to aspire for my daughter's hand after all . . .'

'I had thought of clinical work, sir.'

'Clinical work? What sort of clinical work?'

'In the East End.'

Joseph pursed his thick lips thoughtfully.

'As a stepping stone, perhaps—yes, as a stepping stone. After all, the East End isn't so far from the West End, is it?'

Diana said peevishly:

'Try to persuade him not to go, Father—there must be lots of jobs a doctor can get in Cornwall. Why should he go all the way to London?'

41

'But you don't *want* to stay in Cornwall, do you, Maynard?'

'I'd like nothing better, frankly.'

'Not as a country G.P.!'

'Yes—as a country G.P.'

Joseph uttered a short, contemptuous laugh.

'Well, there's no chance of that in Tresanton. I understand that girl of Peterson's is coming home to partner him. Think she'll be any good?'

'Yes,' Christopher answered quietly. 'I think she'll be very good. For one thing, she's well qualified, and, for another, she's George Peterson's daughter.'

Diana's father began to pick his teeth thoughtfully.

'I'd like to see Sally again—she's my daughter's oldest friend, y'know. A nice kid, I always thought. No side about her—not like *some* folks in these parts.'

But there was more to it than that. Quite apart from the fact that her father had treated his insomnia better than any doctor before, the additional fact that she was Diana's friend was sufficient to earn her a welcome at The Towers. In fact, she was the only real friend Diana had ever had. All his daughter's other friends—the wealthy ones she had met abroad and whom she saw on her frequent visits to London, but never invited to her home, seemed to be kept very much in the background of her life.

'Why don't you invite them to The Towers more often, Diana?' he would ask, and feel baffled by her evasion. It never occurred to him that she was actually ashamed of her ostentatious home.

Once or twice, of course, a few of Diana's friends had come, but he never really felt at ease with them, even though they were the kind of friends he'd always wanted her to make—rich and titled—and he had fully expected that his own wealth would make him acceptable to them. But their rather distant courtesy had left him feeling still an outsider.

But Sally Peterson was different. She never made him feel uncomfortable. It was never necessary, in her presence, to justify himself; to draw attention to his success, or to boast about being a self-made man.

He pushed back his chair abruptly.

'Well, I hope I see her over the weekend— I'd like to tell her that we're looking forward to her coming back for good.'

I'm not, said Diana's expressive glance as she looked across at Christopher. *Not if it means your going away . . .*

What's she like now?' Joseph asked idly. 'Still the plump little frump who used to ride with her father on his rounds?'

'Anything but,' Christopher retorted crisply—to Diana's surprise. 'She's very charming.'

43

This opinion was confirmed as the weekend wore on. He saw her at meal-times, and sometimes in the kitchen when he popped in, between surgeries, to have a cup of tea with Martha. Sally was usually perched upon the table, with her father seated in an old Windsor chair beside the big stove. The atmosphere was contented and companionable. Only a sense of expectancy, a happiness about the future shared by father and daughter, excluded him— and even this Christopher was able to forget when he walked with Sally back from church on Sunday morning.

Her father was tired that day. Christopher checked up on him when, on taking his morning tea, Martha reported that the master wasn't looking quite himself. But there was nothing radically wrong. 'Don't get up till lunch-time,' Christopher advised—and that was how he came to walk across the fields from church, alone with Sally. It wasn't a long walk, but they took it slowly, for they found they had a lot to say; a lot in common.

There were other moments, too, when they talked together. Of their student days; of their hospital experiences. He told her about the Welsh pits and of the gallantry of the men who went down them.

'Not only the miners,' she said gently. 'My father told me how you came to injure your leg. It was lucky for us, of course,' she smiled, 'or we wouldn't have had you to carry on until

44

I came home . . .'

It was only when that moment was mentioned—the moment of her impending return—that restraint crept in and the disappointment which already troubled him seemed intensified.

Once he said, 'It's strange to think that when you do return, I won't be here to greet you.'

'Perhaps we'll meet again.'

'Perhaps.'

(When you come to see Diana? she wondered—but said nothing.)

When they finally said good-bye he held her hand a moment longer than was strictly necessary and said:

'I've a confession to make. Before I met you, I expected someone totally different.'

'In what way?'

'In every way. You're not what I expected, that's all.'

'Better, I hope?' she retorted lightly.

'Much better.' He dropped her hand and they stood for a moment, a little awkwardly, waiting for her father to bring the car to the front door. When it appeared Sally said:

'Well—good-bye.'

'Good-bye, Sally.'

She looked up at him. He was very tall, very broad—not good-looking, like Martin; not handsome a bit. But she knew suddenly that she would never forget him, and wondered

45

why.

'I'm sorry we won't meet again,' she said suddenly, 'but my father says he's quite sure you'll land a very good appointment. He says you can't fail to.'

He gave a lop-sided grin.

'I must thank him for those kind words. Or you, perhaps?'

'No thanks necessary. We both believe it.'

'And I believe I shall be replaced by a very competent young doctor. And I mean that, too.'

The ancient family car halted at the steps.

'Ready, Sally?' called her father.

She answered: 'Coming!' and looked at Christopher Maynard once again. 'Well—good luck!' she said, and ran down the steps. She didn't look back as the car drove through the gates. She didn't want to, because somehow she felt that to do so would only intensify the strange disappointment in her heart; the sense of loss.

They had driven quite a way before she spoke, then she said:

'It's rather sad, isn't it?'

'What, my dear?'

'Meeting people and saying good-bye—like ships passing in the night.'

George Peterson gave his daughter a sideways glance from his wise old eyes.

'That's life, Sally. People come; people go. But sometimes they meet again, you know.'

46

She felt a swift tide of colour flood her face and turned away, studying the countryside with apparent interest. Her father saw too much, perhaps. At any rate, more than she cared for him to see at this moment. It was the first time in her remembrance that she had wanted to hide anything from him.

The old doctor smiled a little to himself and was silent. The train was already in the station. Sally climbed into a third-class compartment and her father placed her suitcase in the rack then stooped and kissed her. They had a few moments before the train pulled out, and he stood upon the platform, looking up at her affectionately. The weekend had done him good; he looked more rested; his lean face had relaxed. Suddenly she put out a hand and touched his cheek.

'What a lovely weekend it has been!' she said.

'Perfect in every way, my dear.'

'And I'll soon be back, so I won't say good-bye.'

'Of course not. It could never be good-bye, between us.'

*   *   *

When Sally had gone, Christopher stood for a while upon the steps of the house, then went inside and shut the door. Somehow, since her visit, the place had changed. Previously it had seemed beautiful, yet a little austere—a bachelor establishment, no more. Now a different imprint was upon it. Sally's imprint. It was there, in the flowers she had gathered from the garden and displayed in colourful groups about the house; in the deep arm-chair where she had sat after breakfast, reading the morning paper—the cushion still bearing the impression of her head; it was in the atmosphere itself; it was everywhere, in a subtle and indefinable fashion. Would that imprint fade and die during the ensuing weeks, he wondered, and revive again with her coming? That, he would never know, because by the time she returned he would be gone— for good.

But there he was wrong: Five weeks later— just a few days before Sally was due to come home and he himself was due to depart, old Doctor Peterson died in his sleep. Quietly and without fuss. As peacefully and contentedly as he had lived.

CHAPTER FIVE

Sally didn't believe it. Her father couldn't leave her so suddenly—snuffed out like a candle in the night. But that was how it had happened, as if a puff of wind had blown out the flame of his heart.

Christopher's voice gave her the facts gently over the telephone.

'He didn't suffer,' he said. 'He couldn't have suffered. He was happy during the weeks following your visit, talking all the time about your return, and then, last night, he went to bed as usual—and didn't wake up.'

She was glad Christopher didn't add the trite advice, given so glibly and so futilely by everyone else: 'Don't grieve for him, my dear.' What else could she do? And somehow Christopher knew that and held his peace.

'He was happy,' he said again. 'Happy because you were coming home to work with him. These last few days he's been positively excited—too excited, perhaps.'

But that was natural enough, his voice implied. When a man has waited years to achieve a certain goal, attainment can be intoxicating. Too stimulating, perhaps, for a heart weakened by years of toil.

'He didn't suffer, Sally—remember that,' Christopher repeated. 'And he *was* happy— remember that, too.'

She stumbled her thanks. There was a brief and potent silence between them, echoing down the miles in silent communication. He wanted to tell her how desperately sorry he was, and could not. He wanted to comfort her, but had neither the right, nor the ability. He was a stranger to her—met briefly and, no doubt, forgotten the moment she returned to

49

London. But he was here, at Tresanton, taking her father's place for the time being. At least, he thought, I can do that and do it well.

'The practice won't suffer,' he assured her. 'I promise you that.'

'I wasn't thinking of the practice.'

'Of course not. I just wanted to let you know that I'd look after things; that I'll do anything I can to help . . .'

'Thank you.'

Her voice was a whisper. He just caught her words before the line cleared, and he knew that she had hung up. The reverberating silence, echoing over miles of space, seemed to emphasise the distance between them. There was a void which he could not span—the void of sorrow and loss.

He knew what they had meant to each other, George Peterson and his daughter, and suddenly Chris felt inadequate, a stranger to devotion, for in his own life there had been nothing like it. Aunt Helen—conscientious and duty-bound—had looked after him well when his own father, an Army man, had been abroad, and his mother, frail and ailing, had found the added burden of a young son too much for her. Scarcely had his father retired from Army life and returned to England, than he died—and in that short time Christopher hardly became acquainted with him.

So devotion such as Sally Peterson shared with her father was an unknown quantity to

50

him—and one he secretly envied. But it shut him out, like an alien viewing unknown territory.

He applied himself diligently to his work, whilst the capable Martha, red-eyed with grief, continued to run the house and Diana made plans for Sally's return.

'She must stay with us until after the funeral,' she said. 'Daddy and I both want her and it will make things easier all round. You can remain at Creek House and carry on the practice, Chris, and anyway, it will be good for Sally to be with us.'

So it was Diana who met Sally at the station. The hospital authorities were sympathetic and understanding, releasing her immediately. 'But if you ever want to return,' the super. said, 'we'll find an opening for you. Remember that.'

Sally thanked him, but thought how unlikely it would be. Her father's work awaited her in Tresanton; their plans would be unchanged. She'd have to apply to the Executive Council for the practice, of course, but that would be a mere formality. After that, she would pick up the threads he had dropped, and carry on. She would still be Doctor Peterson of Creek House, the fourth in the family line. She wouldn't let her father down by failing his dreams and his hopes. What else had she worked for, all these years?

She took the first train she could catch and

there was Diana, waiting for her—looking, Sally noted in the stunned recesses of her mind, as lovely as ever, a striking contrast to the quiet country folk about her. It was always rather surprising to think of Diana living down here in this sleepy part of Cornwall. It seemed the wrong background, somehow. Too unsophisticated. Too lacking in glamour. No wonder she took frequent trips to London.

'Sally, dear . . .'

The cool, scented cheek touched her own. Diana never kissed—not her women friends, at least. Such endearments were not only a menace to make-up, but rather embarrassing —even between old friends. But perhaps she thought some demonstrative action was necessary now, for she put her arms about Sally, briefly, and held her close.

'Darling, you must know how terribly sorry I am!'

'Thank you, Diana.'

Gently, Sally drew away. She didn't want to betray herself here, in full view of the sympathetic eyes of the stationmaster, ticket-collector and porter, who had known her from childhood and loved her father well. She wanted to get home, to Creek House, as quickly as possible.

'It was good of you to meet me,' she said mechanically as they walked towards the barrier.

'Good gracious, what did you expect? I'm

52

your friend!'

Sally experienced a warm rush of gratitude. It was good to feel, at a moment like this, that people cared about her. It made her home-coming less break. The thought of returning to a house bereft of her father's gentle personality was painful to contemplate. Not to see his welcoming smile upon the station platform had been bad enough; to turn in at the gates of her home, to open the front door, to mist his outstretched hands and well-loved voice would be even worse . . .

She pulled herself together firmly, and walked with Diana out into the station yard. One of the Langdon cars stood there—magnificent, of course. 'Mine's gone in for an overhaul,' Diana said casually—which explained the luxurious saloon with an impeccable chauffeur at the wheel. Only in her own expensive sports car did Diana drive about the countryside—at a speed which, said old Martha, was a menace on the narrow Cornish lanes.

As she stepped into the softly-upholstered interior, Sally knew it was ridiculous to recall the worn seats of her father's much-used vehicle; illogical to prefer it. And yet she did. To glide smoothly out of the cobbled station yard, instead of bumping merrily over it, only emphasised the difference between this and her normal home-coming.

Sally felt the prick of tears behind her eyes.

If only Chris Maynard could have brought the family car to meet her, she thought, how much nicer it would have been! But that, too, was ridiculous. He was carrying on the practice, so how could he spare the time?

It was good of him to hold the fort. He'd promised to do so until everything was settled—the funeral, her father's affairs; the transfer of the practice, too, she assumed. Bother red tape and formalities! Sally thought suddenly. If she could only plunge into work right away, how much better it would be!

If she could walk into her father's surgery, sit at his desk, meet his patients one by one and continue where he had left off, it would be more than an antidote to her grief. It would be the immediate fulfilment of their dreams.

Diana glanced briefly at Sally and away again. The girl's face was drawn and pale—she'd taken the shock badly, of course. That was only to be expected. For a fleeting moment Diana felt a swift envy—a suprising envy—for an understanding such as Sally had shared with her father was an unknown quantity to her, too. Sometimes Diana felt that she and Joseph were poles apart—but that wasn't her fault, was it? His business had come first always—human relationships second.

Sally became aware that the car was turning away from the direction of Creek House. Why? Diana sensed the query and said at once. 'Darling, you're coming to us, naturally.'

A sharp pang of disappointment shot through Sally. It was kind of Diana to take her back for lunch, of course, but she'd so much rather go straight home and eat a simple meal in the kitchen with Martha. She felt a need for the woman's comforting presence. She mustered a smile and thanked Diana, but when the car drew up at the steps of The Towers and the chauffeur followed with her suitcase, she stood still abruptly.

Diana said gently: 'You're staying with us, Sally. Where else could you stay?'

'At home! Naturally—at home!'

'But Christopher is there. A bachelor, living alone . . .'

The implication suddenly made Sally laugh.

'But that's ridiculous, Diana! Martha is there, too. If you think a chaperone is needed . . .'

The bluff voice of Joseph Langdon cut across her words. He was striding down the long hall to meet them, his heavy footsteps echoing loudly, his voice booming.

'Sally, my dear—it's good to have you with us! Welcome to The Towers!'

(Really, thought Diana contemptuously, he might just as well sound a fanfare!)

Nevertheless, she reached up and kissed her father's florid cheek. He expected it and, after all, it was never wise to antagonise one's bread-and-butter, especially when accompanied by lashings of jam.

'Now where's your luggage, Sally?' Joseph

regarded in some surprise the single suitcase a servant was carrying upstairs. 'God bless my soul! Is that all you've brought with you?'

'It's all I've got,' Sally admitted with a smile. 'A house-physician doesn't need a lot of clothes, you know.'

But that didn't satisfy Joseph. His idea of comforting a heart-broken girl was to be over-genial; to take her out of herself.

'But surely you need plenty for stepping-out in London? Don't tell me a young girl like you hasn't been hitting the high spots every night?'

Sally forced a smile.

'A young doctor in the East End doesn't get much chance to do that. Of course, there were hospital dances and such things—and I made friends, but they were mostly struggling doctors, as impecunious as myself.'

'Wrong—all wrong!' barked Joseph. 'Women were never meant to work—especially young women, my dear. They're meant to be pretty and decorative, and to be an asset to a man in his home. Much as I respected your father, and mourn his loss, I never agreed with his ideas for you. I may be old-fashioned, of course,' (this was said in a tone which implied that he couldn't possibly be) 'but the idea of women going in for medicine has never appealed to me—any more, I suspect, than it appealed to Martin Penfold.'

'I'm sure you're wrong. Martin always understood my desire to go in for medicine—

56

and approved it.'

'Nonsense, my dear, nonsense! He may have pretended to, of course, for your father's sake—but now you'll marry him and settle down like a sensible girl, and leave the health of Tresanton in the hands of young Doctor Maynard. I gather he wants to stay.'

He didn't see Sally's startled glance—only his daughter's swift frown as she said: 'Really, Father, must we discuss Sally's future now? Give the Poor girl a chance for a wash-and-brush-up before lunch. I've put you in the blue room, Sally. I thought you'd like that. It has your favourite view of the creek . . .'

Sally made no answer; she was too dumbfounded to speak. So they didn't think she'd apply for the practice, after all. They thought she'd give up the whole idea, now her father had died, and marry Martin—as everyone had always expected her to. Marrying Martin was her own concern, and it was connected with the future, not the present.

What had been going on here in Tresanton, she wondered suddenly? What plans had been concocted behind her back? For the first time in her life she felt the uneasiness of suspicion. She had to remind herself forcibly that these people were her friends and that her happiness was their only concern; she would be ungrateful indeed if she forgot that. But she had a sudden sense of urgency—an urgency sharpened by fear. Did Christopher Maynard intend to apply for the practice, too? Surely not—oh, surely not! But the sooner she saw him and asked him outright, the better.

Joseph Langdon's pudgy hand held out a glass to her. 'Drink this, Sally—it'll do you good. You look all in after your journey.'

But it wasn't the journey which had upset her; it was alarm, sharp and poignant.

Joseph regarded her with genuine concern. The poor kid, he thought. She looks absolutely cut-up. But she'll be all right, of course—Martin Penfold will see to that. The best thing she can do is to marry the fellow as soon as possible—as Diana had said at breakfast only this morning.

The drink was strong and stimulating. Joseph was right—it did Sally good. As she went upstairs with Diana, she felt already less tired; the fatigue of her journey gradually seeping out of her. She'd caught an early morning train—a slow one—because she'd been too impatient to wait for a later and faster one.

But little had she dreamed that she wasn't going home—not straight home to Creek House. A sense of being trapped descended upon her; a feeling that life was being organised for her and that unless she fought, and fought hard, the tide would be too strong to withstand.

Diana linked her arm in Sally's and said gently: 'I wanted you to come here, Sally, because I honestly thought it would make you happier at a time like this.'

Sally's reaction was swift—a feeling of guilt, mixed with gratitude.

'It was sweet of you, Diana!'

And she meant it: Diana obviously thought her unhappiness would be emphasised at Creek House; she wanted to help her, to lighten her load, so it would be kinder to stay at The Towers, whether she wanted to or not. She couldn't abuse such hospitality by refusal. As for Joseph Langdon's advice about the future—she could ignore that. He was the kind of man accustomed to organising things—and people. Accustomed to dictating. And Diana, at least, hadn't agreed with what he said . . .

'Did Martha know you were bringing me here, Diana?'

'Of course—and she thoroughly approved.' Diana opened the door of the blue room and held it open for Sally to pass through. It was a lovely room, but she had no eyes for it—only for the view beyond the window; the distant view of the creek, with a mellow old house standing beside it.

Diana continued lightly: 'She said it would do you good to be with friends—that it would take your mind off things. Personally, I believe the old dear was right.'

But Sally was already standing beside the window, staring out at that distant view. A pang of guilt shot through Diana, for she knew full well that her friend would have preferred to go straight home—but she had reasons of her own for wanting to keep Sally away from there. Christopher had talked about her too much since their meeting. Sally seemed to have made an impression upon him, but just what sort of an impression Diana was, as yet, unsure. Anyway, why throw them together? They could have a lot in common, those two, so why foster it?

Besides, Diana had dreams of her own; dreams which had sprung into being since meeting Christopher.

She crossed the room and stood beside her friend. As she expected, Sally's glance was focused upon Creek House, whose walls, covered with Virginia creeper, glowed like amber against the deep blue waters. There was a peace and serenity about the place which The Towers would never achieve, no matter how much money her father lavished upon the place.

One jutting wing of Diana's home was out-thrust beside them, not turreted and proud, as Joseph saw it, but theatrical and overdone. Sally's eyes glanced towards it accidentally, then went back to the distant view, and Diana said abruptly:

'Ghastly, isn't it? The Towers, I mean. But so typical of Father. He must always advertise himself, and, of course, poor lamb, he hasn't a scrap of taste!'

Sally didn't know what to say. Diana's thinly-veiled contempt for her father always made her feel uncomfortable. It was true that Joseph Langdon was a showman, but he had been a generous—indeed, an indulgent—father to his daughter, educating her as he himself had never been educated and, as a result, placing a barrier between them which now bewildered and hurt him.

'I think your father is a wonderful person, Diana. Look at what he has achieved!'

'Oh, I know, darling—and I'm glad of it, of course, because I should have hated to be the daughter of a poor man. All the same, Creek House has far more dignity and beauty than this place will ever have. I'd rather live there than here.'

There was a note of wistfulness in her voice which Sally had never heard before. She turned to her in surprise, and said:

'You can't mean that.'

'I do mean it. People don't realise—certainly Father doesn't—just how simple my desires really are. Except Christopher, perhaps. He knows I'd be happier in a small country house than in a mansion like this.'

For how long? Sally wondered spontaneously, but checked the thought.

Diana's eyes lingered upon the distant house. Was Christopher there now, seeing patients in the surgery, or was he out upon his rounds? She glanced briefly at the neat,

61

diamond-studded wrist-watch which her father had given her for her twenty-first, and thought: 'No—he'll just be returning home for lunch. Martha will serve it to him in solitary state in the dining-room. But why should he continue to live in solitary state? Why shouldn't *he* apply for the practice—and get it? Then a wife would be an eventual need—even an immediate one.

Expectancy quickened within her, and to conceal it she turned away from the window abruptly and walked towards the door.

'See you at lunch, Sally—and don't forget, Martin is coming, too.'

'I'm glad,' Sally answered. And she was. Her heart warmed at the prospect of Martin's companionship—he had been part of her life for so long and any link with that life, in this unhomely magnificent place, would make her brief stay easier. Quite apart from that, she'd be glad to see Martin for his own sake.

At the door, Diana paused and looked back at her.

'Sally—why don't you marry him?'

Don't push me! Sally thought involuntarily. *Let me lead my own life. Don't plan for me or make arrangements. Leave me alone, Diana!*

She gave her friend a light, non-committal smile and crossed to the wardrobe. Already an unseen maid had unpacked her few possessions; her one good suit, her few dresses, her travelling coat—they hardly filled the vast cupboard. At random Sally took down her housecoat and turned towards the bathroom.

'All right—be a clam!' Diana said laughingly. 'You always were, anyway.'

Sally turned to her in surprise, her hand upon the door knob.

'How little you know me after all, Diana. Surely you've realised, after all these years, that I'm just plain shy? Stupidly, embarrassingly shy when it comes to discussing my own affairs. It's only during these hospital years that I've thawed out a little.'

'They've certainly changed you,' Diana admitted, 'and for the better, I must admit.'

Sally laughed.

'Thanks!'

She went into the bathroom and shut the door, aware of an atmosphere, a tension between them. It's my imagination, she thought as she striped and tubbed. I'm a bit overstrung at the moment. I must pull myself together. I can't accept people's hospitality— even when it's thrust upon me—with ill-will. But oh, how I was looking forward to going home!

Diana went thoughtfully downstairs. Did she really think Sally had changed for the better? Wouldn't she really have preferred her to remain as she used to be—homely and malleable; the admiring little friend so easily dominated and led? All her life she had followed Diana's leadership; right from childhood into girlhood, and even into young womanhood, but now Diana had the uneasy feeling that Sally had changed; that she required more careful handling; that she had become too self-reliant and independent for her liking. And that wouldn't do, at all. Not if things were to work out as she, Diana, planned . . .

CHAPTER SIX

Martin was early for lunch—which didn't surprise Diana in the least. She gave him a mocking little smile and said: 'Sally will be down soon!' and succeeded, as usual, in making him feel uncomfortable.

He never felt at ease with Diana, not merely because she was the daughter of the richest man in the neighbourhood, and his most important client, but because she seemed to faintly deride him. He could never think why. Other people in Tresanton didn't. Sally didn't. But Diana seemed to find his native reserve amusing. He sensed a patronage, too, which he resented.

Of course, she was spoilt. Spoilt and wilful. But she was a good friend to Sally and he had to remember that, even though he would have preferred Sally to stay at his parents' house

64

during this unhappy time, then it would have been unnecessary to come all the way to The Towers to see her. He would have been on the spot to comfort her; to relieve her of anxiety and worry.

Visiting her at The Towers depressed him. He never felt at home in the place and he couldn't imagine Sally doing so, either. She was too simple; too ordinary. But Diana had gone ahead in her own high-handed way and brought her here—for the best possible motives, of course. He reminded himself stoically that the important thing was Sally's happiness just now, and that his own desires should come second.

But not for long, he thought with satisfaction. Now that Doctor Peterson had died, there was no reason at all why she shouldn't marry him at once. He hoped she would give up the idea of practising as a doctor, for there was no longer any need to consider her father's dreams, or to humour his wishes.

Besides, the practice wouldn't be hers; she couldn't inherit it. She'd have to apply to the Executive Council, and surely it wouldn't be worth her while going through all the red tape and formalities—especially when there was already a perfectly capable doctor 'in possession,' so to speak!

So, as far as the future went, Martin felt complacent. Only the present moment discomforted him, for he felt Diana's faintly concealed scorn and writhed beneath it. She knew he was impatient to see Sally, and for some reason it entertained her. She liked him to be kept waiting. She was enjoying herself, lolling in a deep, elegantly upholstered armchair, with one long leg crossed over another, regarding him with negligent amusement. Why? he wondered. Because I am the only man in these parts who isn't her abject slave?

As if sensing his thoughts she chuckled lazily and said:

'You're afraid of me, aren't you, Martin?' as if that explained everything. And the trouble was that it did. He could never yield to a girl like Diana because she was too glossy, too sophisticated, too elaborate altogether, so that he could never relax, or be at ease with her. Not like Sally, he thought fondly, who was so much a part of his life that he couldn't picture it without her.

'Never mind,' Diana purred lazily. 'Sally's back—for good. And the best thing you can do is to marry her as soon as possible. Frankly, I consider you're the perfect husband for her and what could be more suitable than a match between two people, born and bred in Tresanton—the son and daughter of two local professional families? It's ideal!'

For once he was in such complete accord with her that he forgot his discomfort and smiled in genuine agreement. A sense of understanding widened between them and the atmosphere eased perceptibly. She even put out a hand and patted his sleeve companionably.

'Dear Martin—you've always loved her, haven't you?'

'Always,' he admitted simply.

'And there isn't any other man in her life— I'm certain of that.'

He was, too.

'And she can't just step into her father's practice,' Diana continued, 'so I'm sure you can discourage her from trying.'

'Will she need discouraging?' he asked in some surprise. 'Now that her father has died . . . ?'

'We-ell,' Diana said thoughtfully, 'it *is* just possible that she might nurse some secret idea of fulfilling his dreams for him, even now. She's an idealist, you know, and idealists are so hard to divert.'

'But what sense would there be in her applying for the practice? Doctor Maynard is already there.'

'Yes—but he would have to be officially appointed,' Diana answered carefully, 'and somehow I don't think he would apply if he thought Sally intended to—and that would be a pity, don't you think, when the people of Tresanton have accepted him and he's running the practice so well? In fact, the more I think of it, the more I'm convinced that for a doctor

67

to be forced to give up his patients to one who knows nothing whatsoever about their cases, right when he's in the middle of treating them, would be absolutely wrong.'

'I imagine the Executive Council would take that into consideration, and appoint him to carry on.'

'But only if he applied!'

'Of course . . .'

'If he *didn't* apply, but left the way clear for Sally, as she probably expects him to, then her application would be the only one and it would all be plain sailing for her. Not . . .' Diana assured him hastily, 'that I don't want it to be, if her heart is really set on it, but personally I don't think it is. I think it is set on you.'

Martin brightened visibly and Diana pressed on:

'And so you see, don't you, how unfair it would be to Christopher Maynard to force him to give up his work to another doctor?

'On the other hand, some people might consider it unfair to Dr. Peterson's daughter if she were denied the chance of following in his footsteps. After all, everyone knows that was the old man's ambition. And, of course, there's the Peterson tradition; Tresanton is accustomed to seeing the name on the brass plate at Creek House.

'But if she married you—and she will, of course—her name wouldn't be Peterson any more, would it? None of the old dears in

Tresanton would expect her to work after she was married. They still cling to the woman's-place-is-in-the-home idea . . .'

'And so it is,' Martin said.

Diana's thin eyebrows raised.

'Coming from you, that surprises me. I thought you were not averse to Sally becoming a doctor.'

'I wasn't averse to her qualifying, although I must admit that I don't really consider medicine a woman's sphere. Nursing, yes . . . that's different. But I knew her father's heart was set on it and that hers was, as a result. It was for his sake that she worked and studied—I know that.'

'I know it, too. And I know something else—that she'd give it all up the moment she married you and the practice would fall vacant again. She'd only work at it for a time out of a sense of loyalty to her father, and that really wouldn't be fair to the patients, let alone Doctor Maynard.'

So she was anxious for the man to stay, Martin thought shrewdly. Well—he was with her, whatever her motive. Besides, there was a great deal of sense in what she said.

'You think I should dissuade Sally from applying for the practice?' he said.

'No, I think you should persuade her to marry you.'

'I've been trying to do that for a long time.'

'There were obstacles—now removed.

69

There's no reason in the world why she shouldn't marry you at once.'

He couldn't see any, either, and, as if sensing his agreement, Diana smiled brilliantly. 'I'm so glad we understand one another better, Martin. It's funny, but we never seem to have had a chance to before.'

'We've never really talked to one another before.'

He felt considerably happier, and regarded her with greater approval. Perhaps he had been a little unjust in his opinion of her; perhaps her attitude towards him had existed only in his imagination. Certainly there was neither condescension, nor patronage, in her manner now. Her smile was friendly and sincere.

'Martin, I'm so glad you're to marry Sally. I couldn't think of a nicer husband for her!'

The sharp ring of the telephone severed the moment. Diana reached out lazily and picked up a white receiver at her elbow, then suddenly she was attentive, and Martin knew he was forgotten.

'Chris!' There was no denying the delight in her voice.

Martin tactfully disappeared through the french windows on to the terrace, wondering if he was right in assuming that there was something really serious between those two. They were seen together a lot—sailing, swimming, playing golf in Maynard's spare time. Certainly, they were very great friends, but no man stayed merely a friend in Diana's life—not for long, anyway.

Why was she so eager for Maynard to stay in Tresanton? Because she was actually in love with him? The idea was surprising, but not impossible, of course. Martin shrugged it aside. It was a matter of complete indifference to him *who* was appointed to the practice, so long as it wasn't Sally, so if Diana wanted his support in discouraging her from applying, she could have it.

Besides, his father's firm—in which he was junior partner—acted for Diana's father legally, so it might be a wise move to be on her side in this matter. Not, Martin hastened to assure himself, that he had any motive but that of winning Sally for his wife forthwith—but all the same, if he wanted to get on (and he did) it would be discreet to maintain a friendship with Joseph Langdon's daughter.

The hot sun beat down upon the wide terrace and Martin withdrew hastily to a canopied garden seat. It was luxurious and comfortable, and from its depths he surveyed the magnificent garden of The Towers with frank appreciation. Whoever designed these grounds obviously hadn't allowed Joseph to poke a finger in the pie; everything was harmonious and restful. Here he *could* relax—and did.

The pre-lunch cocktail Diana had given him gradually imparted a pleasant, mellowing

71

effect and Martin closed his eyes drowsily. She wasn't so bad, after all. In fact, when you talked to her she was really quite nice—and it was gratifying to know that she was on his side. He wasn't sorry, after all, that Sally was staying here, for Diana would obviously encourage her to marry him.

Of course, he thought reasonably, Diana's true motive might be prompted by friendship and a sincere concern for her friend's future. The fact that she wanted young Doctor Maynard to stay in the vicinity could have nothing to do with it, for she was perfectly capable of tiring of him in a week, as she had tired of others. Besides, what real interest could she have in a mere G.P.? The fellow couldn't possibly compete with other men of her acquaintance—not financially, anyway.

So Martin relaxed, satisfied that he wasn't really complying with any secret plans of Diana's. He didn't want to do that. All he wanted was to marry Sally and, as Diana said, the sooner the better.

Diana's voice drifted out to him intermittently. The first undisguised pleasure had given way to a slightly peevish note.

'Yes,' she was saying, 'of course she's arrived.'

Martin dozed. He'd been in court all morning and an exhausting session it had been. A good lunch and a quiet half-hour with Sally—if he was lucky enough to get it—would put him right again. Meanwhile, it was pleasant to laze here in the shade . . .

Diana glanced over her shoulder and saw, through the open windows, his long, well-tailored figure lounging at ease, apparently asleep. Beneath her annoyance the thought registered that Martin was always meticulously groomed—a little too precise and orderly for her liking. Chris, now, was different. He could appear very well turned out when the occasion demanded, but for the most part he drove around the countryside in a well worn tweed suit which had the uncanny ability of putting his patients immediately at ease. Of course, she thought remotely, when he was successful and sought-after—as she intended that he should be—the country tweeds would be replaced by the costly man-about-town clothes more suitable for the Harley Street physician he would one day become, but, meanwhile, that well-worn tweed suit was somehow lovable, and very much in character.

'Diana . . .'

His voice echoed down the line abruptly.

'Yes?'

'I thought you had gone . . .'

I might as well have gone, she thought furiously, if you only rang to inquire whether Sally had arrived. However, she answered amiably:

'No—I'm still here.'

'Well, listen—I don't want to bother Sally at

73

a time like this, but there are things of her father's to be gone through.'

'Martin will handle all that. He's her solicitor.'

'I meant his personal things.'

'I expect she'll come to Creek House some time and see to those.'

There didn't seem anything more to say. Christopher began to wish he hadn't telephoned, but both he and Martha were concerned for Sally—Martha especially, who was obviously yearning to comfort the girl and convinced that no one could do it but herself. 'I wish she hadn't gone to The Towers,' she'd said only this morning, 'although I expect Miss Diana was right to take her there. There are too many reminders of her father here and it might be distressing for her, until after the funeral.'

He knew Martha was only trying to comfort herself in a roundabout way; that she thought, as he did, that Sally was well able to stand up to pain and loss. She was a girl with character and courage; not a girl to be cosseted and protected. But Diana's thought for her had been a kind and considerate one and, taken all round, perhaps for the best after all.

He was just about to hang up, when from the other end of the line he heard a door opening and shutting, and Sally's voice. He guessed that she had just entered the room.

'Is she there?' he asked. 'If so, I'd like to

have a word with her.'

'I shouldn't bother her now, Chris. She's had a long journey, and she's tired.'

'I won't keep her a moment.'

Diana covered the mouthpiece with her hand and turned to Sally.

'Christopher's on the line. He has time for a brief word with you, provided you make it a quick one. There are things of your father's to go through, apparently. He and Martha wonder when you will be free to deal with them.'

Through the open french window Sally saw Martin's reclining form.

'Tell Dr. Maynard I'll be coming down to Creek House this afternoon, immediately after lunch.' (As if I could stay away! she thought, as she walked out on to the terrace towards Martin.)

She heard Diana speak into the telephone, and a minute later the ping of the bell as she replaced the receiver. Diana didn't follow her friend on to the terrace. She lit a cigarette and stood for a moment frowning thoughtfully. All that talk about going through Dr. Peterson's things was nonsense, of course. That wouldn't be necessary immediately. The whole thing seemed to be a thinly veiled excuse to speak to Sally, and she didn't like it at all. She had her own plans as far as Christopher was concerned, and they were strictly connected with herself.

Diana wasn't a ruthless girl. She was just naturally spoilt and wilful and, having always had her own way, saw no reason why she shouldn't continue to. And she was quite genuine in her belief that by far the best thing for Sally to do was to marry Martin and give up all idea of being a doctor. And then, of course, Chris need have no scruples about applying for the practice.

The trouble with Christopher was that he was a little too honest and upright for these days. He wouldn't dream of competing with Sally if she really hoped to step into her father's shoes, and that meant that the position would be quite unchanged. He would still go away, and she might even lose touch with him. Such an idea appalled Diana.

But if Sally married Martin, as everyone had always expected her to, then Chris could remain and everything would be neat and tidy and exactly as she, Diana, would like it.

She was glad she had had that little session with Martin. They were allies now, and that might be useful.

Supremely confident, Diana had no doubt at all that Sally really would marry Martin sooner or later, for, as far as she knew, no other man had ever looked at her—but, of course, she might still have some lingering idea about fulfilling her father's ambitions. So it was up to Martin to discourage her, and up to she, her best friend, to abet him.

Sally experienced her usual feeling of pleasure at the sight of Martin. It was even more emphasised at this moment, for it brought a feeling of homeliness to her which was lacking in this elaborate house.

At the sound of her step he wakened with a jerk and, jumping to his feet eagerly, came towards her. He took both her hands.

'Darling, I can't tell you how terribly sorry I am about your father. But, at least it was over quickly and he didn't suffer.'

'So Christopher told me,' she answered.

He frowned a little at that, jealous because Christopher had got in before him. It was *his* right to comfort Sally—no one else's.

He put his arms about her and kissed her. She was quite passive, and this he mistook for a natural acceptance—which pleased him.

'Sit down,' he said, and urged her into a garden seat.

She was pale and tired, which wasn't surprising in the circumstances.

'I'll get you a drink . . .' he began.

'Don't bother, Martin. I don't want one.' She looked up at him and smiled. 'I can't tell you how glad I am that you're here.'

'Where else would I be?' he asked simply.

'Did you wangle the invitation to lunch, then?' She laughed a little and Martin, always anxious to say and do the correct thing, answered hastily:

'Good heavens, no! I wouldn't dream of

77

inviting myself to lunch anywhere—especially to The Towers. Diana rang me up and invited me.'

'I'm glad she did,' Sally assured him.

'So am I, although I must admit I don't usually feel at ease in this place.'

'Usually?' she echoed. 'Does that imply that today, for some reason, you do?'

She was a little too perceptive. He thought guiltily of his conversation with Diana. And yet, why should he feel guilty about it? It was the first time they had ever talked together with any degree of understanding or sympathy and since that was the reason for his feeling at ease now, he should be glad of it, not ashamed.

But what had really been behind Diana's sudden approach? She had never shown any particular friendship for him before, and the invitation to lunch he had assumed to be for Sally's sake—and so it was, of course. Martin's legal mind didn't like to be troubled with emotions or hidden meanings or ulterior motives. He liked everything cut and dried. That was why he was anxious to get this matter between Sally and himself settled as quickly as possible—and, as Diana said, there was really no reason why it shouldn't be now.

He decided to waste no further time.

'Sally, last time you came down, I asked you to marry me, and you refused because of your father.'

He was quite unaware of an imperceptible

78

stiffening in her attitude, a sudden guardedness, and blundered on: 'Well, now your father is gone there's no need, is there, to consider him any more?'

The glance she turned upon him was startled.

'Martin, you can't really mean that! You can't imagine that, because Father has died, all we planned together—he and I—should die with him!'

'But there's no need—'

She cut him short abruptly. 'The need is a great as ever before.'

'I can't see why,' he said stubbornly. 'It was your father's whim that you should become his assistant.'

Sally sat up with a jerk.

'His whim! Oh, Martin, how can you say such a thing! I thought you understood—you always *seemed* to understand . . .'

He hastened to reassure her. 'Of course I understood, so long as he was alive. I know he dreamed about you working at his side— taking over where he left off, and all that sort of thing.'

Sally said quietly: 'He *has* left off, Martin. He has left off suddenly and abruptly. Does that mean that I should drop all his plans, just as suddenly and abruptly?'

He sat down beside her and took her hands in his.

'But no one will expect you to even try to do

79

his work, Sally. Besides, how could you? You're not experienced enough.'

'I am experienced enough,' she said stubbornly. 'I've been house-physician at St. Mark's for two years and that was sufficient, in Father's opinion, to qualify me for the job of his assistant, and in *my* opinion it's sufficient to qualify me to take his place. You know perfectly well that St. Mark's wanted me to stay on, and if the super. thought I was good enough for that, I'm certainly good enough to be the new Dr. Peterson in Tresanton.'

He said triumphantly: 'But you won't be Dr. Peterson, darling, when you're married to me!'

He was surprised to realise that he was quoting Diana's words, not his own. 'Anyway,' he added briskly, 'you can't just step into the practice, you know.'

'I'm perfectly aware of that. I shall have to apply to the Executive Council, but that's only a formality.'

'And if they don't appoint you?'

'Why shouldn't they?'

He could see that the very idea appalled her—that it hadn't even entered her head.

'Well,' he said dubiously, 'another doctor might apply, too.'

'Another doctor? But there isn't another doctor in Tresanton!' A thought flashed through her mind—a thought which had obviously not been there before. 'Except Dr. Maynard, of course—but he came as Father's

80

locum. He was due to leave, anyway. And besides, he couldn't . . . he wouldn't . . .'

'Why not?' Martin asked levelly. 'Everyone knows him now. He's been accepted by the village people. They like him very much, I'm told. He's a good doctor. He knows their cases. He's been treating them. It isn't always wise to change boats amid-stream, you know.'

Sally's mouth set stubbornly.

'The people of Tresanton know me, too. They've known me since I was born. I can take over their cases—I'm perfectly confident of that—and the only thing that would deter me from doing so would be the possibility of their not wanting me, and that I just won't believe.'

He had to admit to himself that he couldn't believe it, either. He knew perfectly well that the village folk were looking forward to Doctor Peterson's daughter coming back; that everyone in the place was acquainted with the old doctor's ambition to have his daughter working at his side. She'd be the fourth generation of the family to administer to the medical needs of the village and, in a community as deep-rooted as this, tradition meant a lot.

All the same, he reminded himself stubbornly, the people had accepted Christopher Maynard. He was popular, well liked, a good doctor, and by far the best idea was for him to continue in the job and for Sally to give up the idea altogether.

She said impulsively: 'Martin, haven't you

any faith in me? Don't you really believe in me as a doctor?'

'I believe in you as a person, as a woman,' he answered. 'Of course, I know you qualified well medically, but somehow I've never been able to think of you as a doctor, only as yourself—the girl I want to marry.'

She was touched, but all the same the answer wasn't really what she wanted.

He said gently: 'I love you, Sally, you know that.'

She did—and was glad of it, too. It comforted her. It meant a lot to her. But so did medicine; so did all her years of study and hard work; so did the plans she had shared with her father and had no intention whatsoever of relinquishing now. Martin must be made to see reason, but this was not the time, nor the place—nor the opportunity, in fact, for there was Diana walking along the terrace towards them, saying easily:

'Lunch is ready, and that father of mine gets a little impatient if it's kept waiting.'

So no more was said about marrying Martin and, a little guiltily, Sally was glad of that.

CHAPTER SEVEN

The days that followed convinced Sally that she was right in her decision. The affection and sympathy shown to her by the village people was very deep and real. The village church was packed upon the day that her father was laid to rest in the small churchyard, and in the stunned recesses of her mind she was aware of the genuine sorrow with which the villagers mourned his passing.

George Peterson had been well loved in Tresanton. He had served its people loyally and well, and in the secret corners of her heart Sally resolved that she would do the same.

Everyone was there—the rich and the poor. The entire village seemed to be in mourning, as if its heart briefly stood still, stunned by grief.

Sally sat beside Martha in the little church—the very church in which she had been baptised and in which her parents and her grandparents had been married. Her family ties with this place were deep and strong and abiding.

Martha arrived at the church accompanied by young Doctor Maynard, and throughout the service only the housekeeper's bulky figure divided them. On Sally's other side sat Martin. She was aware of his concern for her, but when Christopher Maynard's glance met hers she felt once again the extraordinary sense of communion she had shared with him at their first meeting. This time it was one of sympathy and understanding, no more, yet beneath it there seemed to be a hidden reassurance which comforted her more profoundly than Martin's sympathy.

She hadn't met Christopher since returning to Tresanton, although she had been down to Creek House several times. But each time he had been absent on his rounds, or out on a case, and she had spent the time alone with Martha, or going through the painful task of sorting her father's possessions. In the meantime she had stayed at Diana's home because it had really been the easiest thing to do and in her present state of mind Sally was not in the mood for resistance or dissension, and Diana's plans, if thwarted, could so easily provoke her.

The situation hadn't been too bad, after all, for with surprising tact both Diana and her father had left her alone at the very moments that she wanted to be.

The village people had lost no time in welcoming Sally back. They had watched her grow up, and were as fond of her and as proud of her as they had been of her father. They appeared to take it for granted that she would take over her father's practice and, having no knowledge or thought of such things as executive councils, assumed that she would simply step into his shoes.

'And when will you be taking over, Miss Sally?' they asked. 'The sooner the better as far as the village is concerned. Not that we won't be sorry to see young Doctor Maynard go. A nice young man, he is—and a good doctor, too. Your father always said so, and he ought to know.'

Sally agreed that her father had thought highly of young Doctor Maynard.

'Now why don't you share the practice between you?' old Mrs. Cruwys suggested. 'After all, Doctor Maynard's been helping your father, and I must say he's done my arthritis a power of good.'

'He came as my father's locum,' Sally explained, 'to help him when he was ill. The practice isn't really big enough for two doctors. Besides, Father always said that Christopher Maynard was worthy of better things.'

'Better than being doctor to Tresanton!' the old lady protested. 'What *could* be better than that, Miss Sally?'

Sally checked a smile. 'Well, he could get a job in London for instance. I believe he has that in mind.'

'Then I'm disappointed in him—deserting us folk for the likes o' *them*! There are plenty of doctors in London. Anyway, young Doctor Maynard should stay right here and work beside you. That's what I say!'

'He wouldn't want to,' Sally laughed, 'even if there were enough work for the two of us.'

It wasn't until after the funeral that she spoke to Christopher—and then only briefly. He murmured a conventional greeting, but didn't waste time on expressions of sympathy.

Somehow they weren't necessary. She knew what he felt, without being told.

Martha's voice said beside her: 'You'll be coming home soon, I hope, Miss Sally. The place doesn't seem the same without you.'

'As soon as I can make my excuses to Diana and her father,' Sally replied.

She was sure that that would be quite easy now the funeral was over. After all, there were lots of things to be attended to at Creek House, and the best antidote for pain was work, and plenty of it. So the sooner she submitted her application to the Executive Council, the better. Of course, there would be a lot to learn. Christopher Maynard would have to go over the cases with her and show her just what he had done to date.

As if sensing her thought, he said: 'My time's at your disposal, Sally—any time you care to name, I'll go through things with you.'

So he didn't intend to apply for the practice, after all, Sally thought with relief. I wonder why I feared that he would?

He wasn't the sort of man to do a thing like that, and although she would be as sorry as everyone in Tresanton to see him go, she knew that this step in his life would only be a step upwards, after all, and in robbing him of the chance to continue at Tresanton, she was not placing any stumbling block in the path of his career.

Her heart felt lighter at once, and the

strange sense of guilt which lingered there—provoked, perhaps, by the knowledge that he was well-liked in the village and might even be missed by some of the people—left her.

She said impulsively: 'I shall be very sorry to see you go, Chris-everyone will.'

He thought to himself: I shall be sorry to go, too—and that's putting it mildly. There's nothing I'd like better than to take George Peterson's place. But how could I possibly do such a thing—especially now?

He knew that he stood a very good chance of being appointed to the practice, should he care to apply for it. After all, possession was nine points of the law—or so they said! And if he thought for one moment that Sally was likely to abandon her original plans, he'd have no hesitancy in doing so. But he had to respect the old man's wishes—Sally's too. He liked her too much to want to hurt or disappoint her.

Martin suddenly appeared at her side, possessively taking her arm and leading her away towards his car. The gesture vaguely irritated Christopher, although he knew he had no right to feel that way—no reason for it, either. Sally's father had told him that she would eventually marry Martin, so the man's possessiveness was excusable.

Diana's voice said lazily: 'Can we give you a lift, Chris?'

He was surprised to see her there. He hadn't noticed her in the church, and he couldn't imagine funerals being much in her line. He was a little ashamed of the thought, for, after all, he knew Diana better than most people—or had come to during the last few months. Her brittle veneer hid a greater depth of feeling than others seemed to realise.

He saw Joseph Langdon waiting impatiently beside his opulent car.

'I think I'd rather walk, Diana. I've half-an-hour to spare before going out on my rounds.'

'Then I'll walk with you.'

She waved a casual good-bye to her father, then linked her arm in Christopher's and turned away with him. They were half-way down the lane when Martin's neat black saloon car passed them.

Diana said: 'You know Sally's going to marry Martin, don't you?'

'I know she's going to marry him eventually,' Christopher acknowledged.

'A little sooner than that, I think. They plan to marry at once.'

That startled him.

'Are you sure?' he asked quickly.

'Quite sure. Martin told me himself, only the other day.'

Well, why shouldn't they? Christopher thought. What difference did it make? They could live at Creek House and Sally could still run the surgery.

As if sensing his thoughts, Diana said: 'So there's no reason why you shouldn't apply for the practice now, is there, darling?'

'But, Sally—' he began

'She's not going to work. She's going to settle down as a solicitor's wife—quite happily and contentedly. Why shouldn't she? She doesn't have to consider her father's wishes any more.'

He couldn't believe it. He just *couldn't* believe it. He would never have imagined that Sally could abandon her father's dreams just like that. Perhaps he had misjudged her; perhaps the idea of working as her father's assistant hadn't meant so much to her as she had pretended. Had she even pretended for her father's sake? It was possible, of course.

She had loved him dearly, but not dearly enough, apparently, to cherish those dreams of his after he had died.

Christopher felt an unaccountable disappointment; a sense of disillusionment. George Peterson had told him that to serve the village people of Tresanton meant as much to his daughter as to himself, but now it seemed that the old man had been mistaken.

Christopher's sense of disappointment was illogical. It didn't matter to him if Sally Peterson wasn't the idealist he had believed. It didn't matter to him if she married Martin Penfold tomorrow. In fact, it was all the better if she did, from his own point of view.

It seemed that she was ready to abandon her father's ideals at the drop of a hat, so they couldn't have meant much to her, after all—not if she could give them all up for marriage. Her father had intimated that she would continue to practise as a doctor, even after she was Martin's wife, but he had been wrong, apparently.

Christopher was glad that old Doctor Peterson couldn't know of his daughter's change of mind. At least, he had died believing that it was her intention to fulfil his wishes.

Would Sally have changed her mind, Christopher wondered now, if her father had lived? Would she have come home after her two years at St. Mark's Hospital and said: 'I'm sorry, Father, but I am going to marry Martin and give up all thought of continuing as a doctor?' No—she wouldn't have done that, but perhaps she would have played at being the village doctor for a while before giving it up for marriage, and he, to whom the practice had come to mean so much during the last six months, would have quit the job for no purpose whatsoever, for he had no doubt at all that George Peterson would have retained him as his assistant if his daughter had let him down.

Chris had no doubt. either, that if he was to apply to the Executive Council, as Diana suggested, he would stand a very good chance of getting the appointment. So long as he believed that Sally herself intended to apply he wouldn't dream of doing such a thing, but

90

now—and his pulses quickened at the thought—the coast was clear. There was absolutely no reason why he shouldn't stay in Tresanton!

He felt the pressure of Diana's fingers upon his arm and heard her voice saying urgently: 'You will stay now, won't you, Christopher?'

'I'd like to,' he admitted slowly. 'I'd like to more than anything else on earth.'

There was such a depth of sincerity in his voice that Diana, though pleased, was more than a little startled. She couldn't understand why a quiet country practice could appeal to him so much, and thought, complacently, that the chief reason must be herself. After all, he was in love with her. She was confident of that, although he hadn't told her in so many words. But there was a deep mutual attraction between them which was gratifying.

They had reached the creek and, as if by mutual consent, turned and walked across the shingle and sat down upon a jutting rock.

The whole of Tresanton was clustered about the creek, the rows of white and pink-washed cottages rising tier upon tier to the peak of the surrounding hills, capped on the northern side, rather theatrically and a little incongruously by Diana's magnificent home.

But Christopher saw only the simple rows of cottages, and the fishermen on the beach mending their nets, and the narrow streets—more like alleys—climbing up from the

91

harbour wall in flights of steep stone steps. The whole place had a beauty which wrapped itself about his heart and, more than beauty, it had a warmth of humanity, a personality of its own. It was unique and he loved it.

Diana's glance followed his.

'It's a pretty little place, isn't it?' she said, 'You know, I never really realised that before. To me it's always seemed dull, buried alive—especially in winter—but since you came it's taken on a different character altogether.'

He was glad he had been responsible for making her see the place through different eyes.

'It could do with a bit more life about it,' she continued musingly. 'Father has plans for building a big hotel over there on the headland. I really do think that with all the holiday facilities this place has to offer Tresanton could really become a money-making resort.'

Christopher shuddered at the idea. He turned and slipped his arm companionably about her waist and said:

'Then I hope you'll do all you can to dissuade him, my sweet. Too many Cornish places have been exploited—let's leave this one unspoilt, shall we?'

'Whatever you say, darling,' she answered lightly.

She didn't really care what the place was like so long as he was here—so long as they could sail together and swim together and

92

drive into Falmouth or Truro for an evening's entertainment. Plymouth wasn't far away, either, and the shops there weren't bad really—not so good as London, of course, but better than nothing.

Besides, she had her own ambitions for Christopher and if they came true (and why shouldn't they?) Tresanton could be their holiday home—no more.

But all that was in the future and, right now, Diana was only concerned with the present. The important thing was to keep Christopher here. He wanted the practice, his heart was secretly set on it—then why shouldn't he have it? She had always got what *she* wanted and because he meant so much to her she quite genuinely wanted him to have his own way, too.

Diana was still faintly surprised at her reaction to Christopher Maynard. There had been men in her life before, of course, but none had affected her as he did; none had swept her off her feet in quite the same way. She was obsessed by him, and when Diana became obsessed by a thing she never gave up.

As to the future—his future—she had her own plans for that, too. It must be firmly linked with her own. He was a good doctor; a clever and promising one. George Peterson had told her father so, even admitting that he had been lucky to get him as a locum. Unfortunately Chris himself was by no means rich, but what did that matter? She herself had plenty of money, and would always have. It was even lucky, in a way, that Christopher was comparatively poor, otherwise he wouldn't have been forced to look for a locum's job and they would never have met.

He was a man of the future, she was confident of that. Indeed, she was determined that with her father's money behind him, coupled with her own determination as his wife, there would be no limit to Christopher's achievements. He could become the leading physician in Cornwall, serving on the best local hospitals until eventually his name became known farther afield, leading him inevitably to Harley Street.

Oh, there was no limit to her dreams for him, for both of them! She wanted him badly and she wanted Creek House, as well. It was small and charming and full of character—she could make it into a beautiful place. Money would be no object, of course. She would build a loggia outside the drawing-room windows, commanding a lovely view of the creek, and in the hall—the simple, white-panelled hall with which Sally and her father were so well content—she would have a cocktail bar installed and the panelling painted a delicate *eau-de-nil*, or perhaps wedgwood blue, picked out in gold.

It would be a delightful house to live in, and a delightful house to entertain in. She could well visualise herself as mistress of it and, after Chris became the prominent physician she planned, Creek House could become their country home.

One could always arrange life if one went about it the right way, Diana reflected with satisfaction.

'Chris, you *will* apply for the practice, won't you?' she urged. 'There is nothing to stop you now.'

'You're really sure of that?' he asked anxiously. 'I want to be absolutely sure because I wouldn't like to—'

She cut across his words impatiently: 'I wouldn't have told you, if I hadn't been sure! Martin came to see Sally the minute she arrived and the whole thing was settled. Surely, you're not surprised?'

He answered uncertainly: 'I knew they were likely to marry, but not immediately.'

'But with her father's death everything has changed. Don't you see that?'

He did see it, and the whole thing was more than a surprise to him.

'It's strange,' he mused aloud. 'I didn't imagine she'd do a thing like this—abandon her father's ideas, I mean. They meant so much to her—or I thought they did.'

'In her father's lifetime, yes,' Diana admitted, 'but he is dead now. She has her own life to live and you can't blame her for marrying Martin.'

95

'No,' he admitted reluctantly, 'I don't blame her.'

But, all the same, he was aware of a vague disappointment, a regret which troubled him inexplicably.

'I expect they'll have a very quiet wedding,' Diana continued. 'It will have to be, of course, so soon after her father's death.'

'Where will they live?' he asked unexpectedly, as if the thought had just occurred to him—which, indeed, it had.

Diana shrugged.

'Oh, I expect Martin will buy a house somewhere. He's quite comfortably off, you know. His people have been the local solicitors for years and he will inherit everything.'

'Then they won't want Creek House,' he said thoughtfully.

'They won't be able to have it, will they?' she asked swiftly. 'Surely it goes with the practice?'

He laughed. 'Of course not, Diana. The practice is one thing, the house another.'

'But you would want to stay there, wouldn't you?' she asked anxiously.

'If I could possibly afford it, yes. It depends upon what price Sally asks for it.'

'I'll have to find out,' Diana said quickly.

'I shouldn't bother her about that, if I were you. She has a lot on her mind, what with settling her father's affairs, and her approaching wedding. I expect the sale will be

96

put in the hands of an agent, anyway. But I doubt if I'll be able to afford it. I'll have to buy something a little more modest—a cottage in the centre of the village, perhaps.'

'Then you *are* going to apply for the practice?' she said eagerly.

There was a note of urgent excitement in her voice which he couldn't miss. He was a little touched by it and, covering her hands with his own, answered:

'I see no reason now why I shouldn't, do you?'

'None whatsoever!' she cried in delight, 'but I think you should give up the idea of a more modest house. Everyone in Tresanton knows Creek House as the village doctor's. It might be a mistake to change.'

'That depends on whether I can afford to buy it,' he answered.

Nonsense! she thought with secret delight. You won't have to worry your head about that, my poor sweet. I can easily persuade Daddy to give it to us as a wedding present.

But all that could come later.

She said practically: 'I don't think it would give a good impression for a doctor to live in one of the village cottages.'

'As to that, Diana, I'm not the sort of man who sets out to make an impression. The people here have accepted me as I am and I think they'll continue to. If I *am* appointed to the practice, that is.'

97

'You will be,' she answered confidently. 'What is there to stop you?'

Nothing, he thought immediately—absolutely nothing. He could apply now with a clear conscience.

And yet, beneath his elation, disappointment persisted—a disappointment in Sally, who hadn't turned out to be the kind of girl he thought her, after all.

CHAPTER EIGHT

As far as Diana could see, nothing could possibly go wrong, so long as Sally and Christopher didn't meet—at any rate until the question of the practice was settled.

She salved her conscience with the thought that if she hadn't been entirely truthful with Christopher, she wasn't likely to be found out—and, meanwhile, surely Martin would prevail upon Sally to do as he wished? What little help she, Diana, could give in that direction she would unhesitatingly bestow. A little gentle persuasion, perhaps; a word or two here and there. And that would be easy enough so long as she kept Sally here at The Towers for the time being.

So she was a little unprepared for Sally's sudden decision to return home. Sally announced it at breakfast the morning after

98

the funeral and Diana stared at her friend aghast.

'You can't mean it,' she said. 'You can't intend to walk out, just like that!'

Sally coloured. It hadn't been her intention to do anything of the kind, but, put like that, her decision did seem a little abrupt. Even ungrateful.

'But, darling,' Diana rushed on, 'I've been counting on your staying here with me for a few days.' She pouted prettily and cast a pleading glance in her father's direction. 'After all, life's awfully dull here, all on my own.'

That was an open bid for her father's support, and he knew it. But Sally didn't. Somehow she never imagined life being dull for Diana, who always seemed to have so much to do with her time and so many people to spend it with. But perhaps, after all, she was wrong about her. Perhaps the friends she made were not really congenial after all— except Christopher Maynard.

She knew Diana spent a lot of time with him. Martin had told her that—very significantly, it seemed on recollection. 'Of course,' he had said, 'I'm not saying there is anything *between* them exactly, but . . .'

Joseph Langdon's voice cut into Sally's thoughts. As Diana expected, her father had come to her aid immediately. Whatever the girl wanted, she must always have.

'What's the hurry, Sally?' he asked over the

top of his morning paper. 'You've just gone through a trying time, my dear, so why not relax for a few days? Stay here and keep Diana company. You'll be good for each other.'

It was more of a command than a request, Sally felt. It was the great Joseph Langdon speaking—the man whom nobody disobeyed except his daughter, perhaps. As Sally well knew, there were moments when Diana was capable of twisting her father around her slender little finger.

Joseph Langdon gave a satisfied nod. 'I'm glad that's settled,' he said, and went back to his paper.

And it *was* settled, too, Sally thought ruefully. Settled in the way everything seemed to have been since her return. She had a sense of being trapped—and it wasn't the first time that such a feeling had assailed her during the last few days, as if she were being pushed along tracks not of her own choosing.

And yet everything was done with the best possible intentions. These people were her friends, she had to remember that. Their thoughts were only for herself.

Suddenly Joseph Langdon laid his newspaper aside and placed both of his hands, large and broad and hairy, upon the table. It was almost as if he was presiding at a board meeting.

'Now, my dear,' he said. 'About your future—'

'My future?' Sally echoed politely.

'I expect we can leave that safely in young Martin Penfold's hands, eh?'

All Sally's defence mechanism went up at once. She wished that people would leave her alone. She wished they would stop planning for her, thinking for her, as if she was incapable of making any decisions for herself. Did they imagine she had no ideas of her own about her future? Apparently not, for Joseph Langdon continued blandly:

'As for your father's practice, young Doctor Maynard will take that over, so you have nothing to worry about on that score.'

'Doctor Maynard?' Sally echoed. 'But he came as my father's locum—he knew that he had to give up as soon as I came home. In fact, he came on that understanding.'

Diana put in gently: 'But you can't become your father's assistant now, Sally.'

Sally's grey eyes met hers.

'No,' she answered levelly, 'but I can take his place.'

Joseph's bushy eyebrows raised in surprise.

'I take my hat off to you, young lady, if you really believe that.'

'Of course I believe it. Why shouldn't I?'

He waved a pudgy hand. There was something faintly disparaging in the gesture which Sally didn't like.

'You're young, my dear, and inexperienced.'

'Not inexperienced,' she corrected. 'I have

been working in a tough East End hospital, and I couldn't have asked for better experience than that.'

'True, true,' he nodded, pursing his thick lips thoughtfully, but doubtfully. Then he looked at his wrist watch, pushed his chair back from the table and said:

'Ah well, my dear, there's no harm in your trying. I wish you luck, anyway.'

'Wait a minute!' Sally cried.

He turned impatiently at the door. Joseph Langdon didn't like to be hindered. He had an industry to take care of, and a flourishing one at that, to which the white chalk pyramids outlined against the sky in the fields beyond Tresanton, well bore testimony.

'What is it, Sally?' he asked impatiently.

A sudden and unexpected shyness descended upon her.

'Nothing,' she said. 'I just wanted to thank you for having me here; for being so kind.'

He gestured magnificently.

'Stay as long as you like, my dear! It couldn't be too long for Diana, I know that. She gets lonely here, and it isn't surprising, I suppose, so stay and keep her company. I'd appreciate it if you would.'

So the matter was settled. Joseph turned and marched out of the room, his heavy tread echoing upon the stone floor in the vast hall beyond.

'More coffee?' Diana asked sweetly, and

held out her hand for Sally's cup.

Sally didn't want any, but she extended her cup automatically. She felt cornered—an uncomfortable position to be in. More than ever she wished she had gone straight home to Creek House, instead of coming here. And yet somehow she had yielded inevitably to Diana's arrangements.

Hadn't she always done so? Hadn't she always walked like a shadow in Diana's wake? I thought I had grown out of that long ago, she reflected.

Diana's voice was frank and sincere and friendly as she passed the refilled cup back to Sally.

I don't want you to think me interfering, Sally, but after all, we've known each other for a long while. We've grown up very close to one another, haven't we?'

Sally wasn't so sure about that now. They'd been friends, yes—friends for almost a lifetime—but just how close were they at heart?

'Well?' she asked carefully.

'Well—all I wanted to say was that you're not really being wise, you know.'

'Wise?' Sally echoed.

'I mean that if you think you can really tackle your father's practice, that you can take over where he left off, that you can even step into Christopher Maynard's shoes, you're being a little too ambitious, darling.'

Diana saw a flicker of impatience crease Sally's brow.

'That's for me to decide, Diana.'

Her friend shrugged.

'Of course, but if you fail to get the appointment, don't say I didn't warn you.'

'How *can* I fail? No one else will be applying—not unless a doctor from some outlying place has heard of my father's death and I doubt if an outsider would stand much chance.'

'But if Christopher Maynard should apply—'

'But he wouldn't! He isn't going to, I know, because he spoke to me after the funeral yesterday and told me so.'

'Did he?'

'Well—not in so many words, perhaps.' Sally's brow puckered thoughtfully. 'He said he would go over things with me as soon as I had the time—so I'm sure I've nothing to fear from him.'

'I'm glad,' Diana said simply. 'But I must say I agree with Father—you've got guts, Sally, to even try, and I do wish you luck.'

'Thank you, Diana.'

'But I wonder what Martin will say,' Diana continued thoughtfully.

'He knows. I've told him already.'

'And did he like the idea?'

Sally laughed a little. 'Well, let's say he'll get used to it, shall we?'

'You mean, he'll get used to his wife being a

doctor?'

Sally evaded that. 'Perhaps we're going a little too far into the future,' she said casually.

'I hope not. The poor man's waited a long time for you, Sally.'

Sally answered uncomfortably: 'Perhaps he won't mind waiting a little longer.'

'I shouldn't keep him dangling *too* long, darling. No man likes to wait for ever.'

Diana rose and pushed back her chair briskly.

'Let's run into Falmouth, shall we? I've a bit of shopping to do and we can have lunch there.'

It's as good a way as any other to spend the morning, Sally thought as she rose and followed her friend from the room.

On their way upstairs to get their coats Diana said:

'About this application for the practice—I really would think twice before sending it in if I were you, Sally.'

'I don't have to,' Sally replied crisply. 'It's gone in already.'

Diana stopped dead in her tracks.

'You haven't wasted much time,' she said slowly.

'Of course not. Did you expect me to? I know what Father wanted me to do and I want to get ahead and do it.'

Diana laughed uncertainly. 'Well,' she repeated, 'as I said—good luck to you!'

She strolled ahead to her room.

'By the way,' she called over her shoulder, 'I've changed my mind about going into Falmouth immediately. Let's go later. I feel like a sail this morning. The regatta starts next Saturday, and I must get in a bit of practice.'

Sally had forgotten all about such things as regattas.

'Who is crewing for you?' she asked with interest.

'Chris—if he's free, that is. Being Tresanton's one and only G.P. keeps him busy.'

There seemed to be an odd significance in her tone which Sally chose to ignore.

Sally went on to her own room and closed the door. She had one or two letters to write and was glad not to be going into Falmouth after all.

She was half-way through her letters when Diana thrust her head around the door.

'I'm just popping down to the village to see if Chris is free for a practice sail this afternoon. If not, I shall have to call on Jim Trewin. He's usually free when the bank closes, and of course,' she laughed lightly, 'he'd do anything for me! We'll go into Falmouth when I get back.'

From her window, a few minutes later, Sally saw Diana's long low sports car racing down the hill towards the village and wondered briefly if Martin were right when suggesting that there was something more than friendship

106

between her and Christopher. They *were* good friends, that was obvious—but Diana had dozens of men friends and all of them, sooner or later, fell in love with her. So it wouldn't be surprising, would it, if Chris Maynard did likewise?

The thought disturbed Sally—she couldn't think why. From her teens she had watched men fall in love with Diana and had never felt any particular jealousy. At the gawky age—the awkward age which Diana never seemed to go through but which she, Sally, most certainly did—she had felt the natural envy which any unattractive girl feels for a pretty one, but hard work and study and examinations had driven such nonsense from her mind. And then, of course, there had always been Martin to bolster her self-confidence when it threatened to waver . . .

Sally stared musingly before her, thinking with a deep and genuine affection of Martin. She owed him so much; years of loyalty and devotion could not easily be repaid. And he meant a lot to her. If she was in love with anyone it was certainly with him.

But at the thought of marrying him, something within her instinctively withdrew. She wasn't ready for marriage yet—she insisted that was the explanation. She had lots to do; her father's work to carry out; dreams to fulfil. There was time enough for marriage, wasn't there? She didn't have to rush into it.

Nor, she thought mutinously, do I have to be pushed—and that is what Diana and her father, and even Martin himself, seem to be doing right now. Why can't they realise that I can stand on my own two feet, that I don't need a husband to take the place of my father?

All the same, she did feel a little guilty about Martin. She had accepted his love—but, on the other hand, she had given him affection, a deep and sincere and genuine affection. Many people married on much less than that.

But *she* didn't want to. She wanted her affection for Martin to be given a chance to grow; to develop into something deeper and stronger, something tinged with passion. Once he had said: 'I know you don't desire me as I desire you, Sally, but that is only because you've known me all your life. I am sure of that. We were children together, then tennis partners—all that sort of thing—and there is nothing very romantic about a background like that. But if you lived with me, slept with me, shared your life with me, everything would change, I know.'

Perhaps he was right. She even hoped that he was, because somehow she couldn't imagine herself marrying anyone else. Or did she really mean that she couldn't imagine any other man coming into her life?

She felt suddenly depressed and restless and put it down to the unhappiness of recent events. A walk would do her good, she decided and, flinging down her pen, she went out into the garden and down to the main gates.

Diana's car had disappeared from sight, but because it had been heading towards Creek House, Sally turned in the opposite direction towards the centre of the village. She felt the need to reassure herself that people really did want her in her father's place, and after half an hour of visiting the village shops and stopping to chat with people by the way, all her doubts had vanished and she knew in her heart that she had done the right thing, made the right decision. There wasn't a person who didn't express their satisfaction at the thought of her picking up the reins which her father had laid down. Not one who faded to welcome her.

'Of course, it may be hard to think of you as Doctor Peterson at first,' some admitted with a smile. 'To us, you've always been "little Miss Sally," but you're your father's daughter and there wasn't a better doctor than he. We'll miss him badly.'

So shall I, thought Sally. I'll miss his guiding hand, his wise head, his experience and knowledge and patience. There was still so much he had to teach me, and I shall have to learn alone now.

But one thing was certain—the people of Tresanton, even though they'd be sorry to see young Doctor Maynard depart, would be behind her unanimously; believing in her, trusting in her, happy to know that the name of Doctor Peterson would still be inscribed upon the brass plate at Creek House.

She felt better after her walk and went back to The Towers to finish her letter-writing. She had only one more to do and was in the middle of it when Diana returned. There was a secret air of happiness about her, a sort of satisfaction which Sally couldn't help noticing.

'Still writing letters?' Diana commented lightly. 'You put me to shame! Letter-writing is a job I abhor, but you were always a diligent little thing, Sally.'

'I went for a walk in the middle of it,' Sally admitted, 'but I have only this one to finish.'

Diana perched upon the side of her desk. It was an exquisite piece of Sheraton, but Diana had grown up accustomed to such things and treated them, Sally thought, rather negligently.

'And who is it to, Sally?' she mocked. 'A secret lover?'

Sally laughed. 'Nothing so romantic, Diana! To the hospital, that's all.'

'St. Mark's?' Diana asked. 'What are you writing to St. Mark's for?'

'They wanted me to go back. The super. offered me a job, but I turned it down, of course.'

'I don't blame you. Martin wouldn't like his wife to work so far away from home.'

Sally ignored that and continued: 'I just thought they would be interested to know that

I've applied for my father's practice.'

'*And* that you haven't much doubt of getting it?'

'I haven't said that, but between you and me, Diana, no, I haven't much doubt. Perhaps I am a better doctor than you think.' She sealed the envelope and rose. 'Ready to go into Falmouth?' she asked briskly.

But Diana didn't stir. She seemed to be regarding Sally with a kind of secret amusement. There was a trace of a smile about her lips—rather like a cat, Sally thought spontaneously, that had just finished some cream.

'You're looking very pleased about something, Diana.'

'Of course I'm pleased—Chris has promised to come sailing with me for an hour after lunch. I just caught him as he was going out on his rounds.'

Sally regarded her friend thoughtfully. 'You like him, don't you, Diana?'

'Very much indeed.'

More than like him? Sally wondered, and felt instinctively that this was true.

'Well,' she said again, 'I'm ready if you are.'

She turned towards the door and Diana followed her, saying lazily:

'If you're wondering whether we're in love with each other, Chris and I—well, perhaps we are.'

'In that case I am happy for you,' Sally

111

answered evenly, and went ahead down the impressive marble staircase.

Following her, Diana thought: I wonder if you really are, my girl? I had an idea that you rather liked Chris Maynard yourself when you first met him, and I must confess I'm glad I've managed to keep you both apart since you returned.

She was glad about something else as well, something about which she had hurried down to Creek House to reassure herself. Christopher's application to the Executive Council had gone in—he had told her so with a new zest and satisfaction, a confidence which she shared, for she had no doubt at all that he would get the appointment. He was older and more experienced than Sally, and had already proved himself capable of running the practice, so what chance had a fledgling fresh from her first hospital job? Boards and councils and such-like didn't take sentiment into account. They operated from headquarters many miles away and were not concerned with local traditions.

Only one thing had clouded Diana's brief meeting with Christopher.

'And how is Sally?' he had asked.

'Oh, she's fine—not that I see a great deal of her. Martin monopolises her with all the possessiveness of a husband-to-be.'

'I can understand that,' Christopher had answered. 'I must be off on my rounds now,

Diana.'

'What about a sail today?' she suggested impulsively. 'You can't keep your nose to the grindstone *all* the time!'

For Christopher's part, the prospect of a sail had suddenly appealed to him. It might blow away some of the doubts and illogical disappointments which had been troubling him, so he arranged to meet her after lunch and Diana returned to The Towers well satisfied.

Perhaps she had deceived Christopher a little—and Sally, too, for that matter—but it was all in a good cause. By far the best thing Sally could do was to marry Martin, anyway. Why should the poor girl devote herself to work? Hadn't she done enough of that already? It was about time she settled down to the ease and comfort which Martin could offer and if, at the same time, it left the way clear for Chris to achieve what he so badly wanted— and what she, Diana, so badly wanted, too— well, that was probably all to the good . . . and if they found out that she had taken a hand in affairs (which was most unlikely) they would have cause to be grateful to her eventually.

Suddenly Diana felt that she was playing the role of fairy godmother, and enjoying it very much. The fact that she was playing fairy godmother primarily to suit her own ends didn't even enter her head.

CHAPTER NINE

In a way, old Martha was glad that Sally had stayed at The Towers instead of coming home. It was best for the girl, perhaps, although Creek House didn't seem quite the same without her.

Sally began to spend a lot of time at her home, however. Her father's things had to be gone through and she had long sessions in his study, with Martin, settling his affairs—sessions of which Christopher was well aware and which made him feel vaguely like an intruder.

He was aware, also, that Martha wanted Sally home again, but wondered whether the old woman knew that when she did return it wouldn't be for long; that it would only be to prepare for her wedding with Martin.

Somehow he felt that Sally hadn't yet broken the news to the housekeeper, so he said nothing himself. But he began to wish that the decision from the Executive Council would come through—then he would at least feel that the practice was his and he could start afresh. There was a vacant house in the centre of the village—small, but not unattractive—which would suit him well, but of course until the appointment was confirmed he could do nothing.

Diana assured him repeatedly that he couldn't fail to get it; that it was only a formality to be gone through and, because he believed no other doctor had applied for it, he felt this, too, but before he went ahead with the purchase of the village house he very much wanted to know what Sally's plans were, for if she and Martin were not going to live in Creek House, if there were the slightest chance of getting it for himself, he wanted very much to try.

But perhaps Sally and Martin planned to live in it together. Unreasonably, the thought oppressed him.

He avoided Sally whenever she came to the house—he didn't really know why. In any case, running the practice single-handed kept him pretty busy, so his avoidance of her didn't seem deliberate. He loved the work and found it easy to lose himself in it, so his contacts with Sally were necessarily brief.

But Sally, remembering what he had said after her father's funeral, was surprised. She had fully expected him to discuss the practice with her—even to suggest that before taking over she should work with him for a while and so become acquainted with the cases. His reticence, she decided, was probably due to a certain consideration for herself—he knew that she was busy going through her father's things and didn't want to worry her with more.

And then, of course, there was Diana—who

was kindness itself these days. She would call for Sally shortly before lunch and carry her back to The Towers, usually before Chris returned from his rounds, insisting that Sally had done enough for one day and that a trip somewhere in the afternoon, or a game of tennis, or a swim, would be good for her. The Langdons had their own swimming pool and there were long leisurely hours when the two girls lay in the sun, talking desultorily, getting to know one another again—or trying to.

But the more she talked to Diana, the more Sally realised how little she really had in common with her. Their long friendship now seemed to be merely one of those childhood ties which had persisted through the years.

She felt a little disloyal when thinking that, but to find any mental meeting ground with Diana seemed impossible these days. There was the gulf of environment between them, the barrier of riches, the years in which Diana had played and Sally had worked—and so, one day, she made a determined effort to break free from the tentacles of her friend's hospitality. She announced her intention to return home the minute she heard from the Executive Council.

To this suggestion Diana agreed lazily. She was lying on her back in the sun and, yawning a little sleepily, said:

'Of course, darling. I quite understand.'

'The council promised an early decision,'

Sally told her, 'so I should hear any day now.'

Diana sat up and stretched lazily.

'Let me know when you do, Sally. I'll be interested to hear the verdict.'

The letter lay on Sally's breakfast plate the very next morning. She knew at once what it was, and her heart pounded excitedly as she slit the envelope. From now on, right from this moment, she thought exultantly, life would begin again! All her plans and dreams—her father's plans and dreams—were at last to come true. There was nothing to stand in the way of their fulfilment now.

She took the sheet of paper from the envelope, scanned it, and was suddenly still.

Diana glanced across the table and saw that Sally had gone deathly white.

'What's the matter, darling?' she asked in concern. 'Not bad news, I hope?'

Sally's lips moved inaudibly, and the paper fluttered from her numb fingers, falling on to the floor at her feet. She felt sick. Sick and stunned and breathless—as if someone had punched her violently in the stomach.

'Father, I think Sally's going to faint or something!'

Joseph Langdon dropped his newspaper and lumbered round the table, but by the time he reached Sally, she had lifted her coffee cup and was drinking. He heard her teeth chattering against the rim of the cup and said:

'God bless my soul! What's the matter,

117

child?'

The coffee was strong and hot and sweet. Sally drained it, laid the cup down carefully and announced steadily:

'They've turned me down.'

'They? Who's "they?" And what have they turned you down for, anyway?'

Diana stooped, picked up the letter and read the cold brief words expressing the Executive Council's regret that she had not been appointed to the practice of the late Doctor George Peterson.

'They've turned me down,' Sally said again. 'Why, why, *why*?'

She no longer felt stunned, but angry. Angry and disbelieving. She looked up at Joseph Langdon's bulky form, still stooping above her with fatherly concern, and said:

'The council rejected me. They won't let me practise in my father's place—and I want to know *why*.'

He patted her shoulder uncomfortably.

'There, there, my dear, I shouldn't take on so! They've probably appointed someone else.'

'Who else?' she cried. '*Who else*?'

'Why not Chris?' Diana said reasonably. 'Is there any reason why *he* shouldn't be appointed?'

'Every reason! He knew that I was going to apply. When he came as my father's locum it was for six months, no more.'

'Look, darling, he didn't know then that

118

your father was going to die—that the practice would become available.'

Sally pushed back her chair angrily. 'He knew perfectly well that Father wanted me to follow in his footsteps, *and* that I wanted to! That I intended to!'

'Now be reasonable, Sally. He knew that you were likely to become your father's assistant when he was alive, but that was entirely different. So if he did apply for the practice, you can hardly blame him.'

Sally stared at her friend and then said slowly: 'I don't believe that he would do such a thing. He knew—I'm *sure* he knew—just how much it would have meant to my father for a fourth generation of the Petersons to become Tresanton's doctor.' She shook her head emphatically. 'Oh, no, I am sure it wouldn't be Christopher—it must be some outsider, some doctor from a neighbouring town or village. But why should the council appoint an outsider?'

'My dear child,' Joseph said mildly. 'Boards are not concerned with village traditions, and although your family have been medical practitioners here for years, the authorities wouldn't weigh that fact against a man's skill and experience. You're young, Sally. You're fresh from your first house-physician's job. It's obvious that the council just didn't consider you suitable. I don't mean that cruelly,' he added, 'but it's a fact you've got to face up to.

Diana, pour the girl another cup of coffee—
it'll do her good.'

But Sally didn't want another cup of coffee.
She wanted to get down to Creek House as
quickly as possible, and the next minute she
was running from the room, down the long hall
and out into the drive. She didn't stop running
until she reached the gates of her home, and
then she pulled up abruptly.

The morning sun was shining upon its
mellow walls and mullioned windows. There
was a peace and serenity and gentleness about
it which was like balm to her troubled heart.
At least, she thought proudly, this is mine—
and it's something that I shall never give up!

She opened the gates and walked up the
path. Through the window of the breakfast
room Christopher saw her coming, and was
surprised, not only because it was an early visit
but because she was breathless and
dishevelled, as if she had been hurrying. He
sensed at once that something was wrong and,
because of his own particular elation at that
moment, felt a sharp concern for her.

They met in the hall and, without a greeting,
she said:

'The Executive Council has rejected me. Do
you know why?'

He stared at her, unable to speak. She saw
that he was holding a piece of notepaper in his
hand, and there was a familiarity about it
which she recognised at once.

She stared at him in stunned disbelief.

'It isn't true,' she said slowly. 'Not *you*!'

It was one of the worst moments Christopher had ever experienced. He looked at the girl's white face and then at the paper in his hand, and suddenly, instead of being overjoyed and elated, he was embarrassed and ashamed.

'It *is* true, then,' Sally said dully. 'I didn't believe Diana—I didn't believe that you could . . . that you *would* . . .'

He answered awkwardly: 'Why not?'

'Because you knew—*surely* you knew that I would take my father's place? Of course, you knew! He told you of his plans. They were my plans, too—and you knew that.'

'I didn't know that you meant to go through with them now, Sally.'

'You mean you didn't care!' she retorted. 'Why should you? You were "the man in possession" and took advantage of the fact!'

The injustice of her accusation stung him to fury.

'If that is what you want to believe,' he said, 'go right ahead and believe it!'

She hated him. She hated him as she had never hated anyone before. But beneath her hatred was a hurt that she would not acknowledge—a hurt because he, of all people, had done this to her. She had liked him, trusted him; she had even been aware of him in a potent and a disturbing way. But any

121

attraction that he might have had was now completely forgotten.

'Tell me, Doctor Maynard,' she said quietly, 'do you like this house?'

'Of course, I like it,' he answered shortly. 'Who could fail to?'

'And you would like to continue in practice here, I suppose, because this has always been known as the house of the village doctor? Well, that's another tradition that will die out now, because no matter how much you may hope to get Creek House, Doctor, you never will!'

'I didn't really expect to,' he answered reasonably. 'I thought it likely that you would continue to live here after you married Martin.'

'Martin?' she queried shortly.

'Your father told me you would eventually marry him.'

'That,' she said stiffly, 'is beside the point. The point is that you are trespassing upon my property, Doctor Maynard, and I must ask you to leave at the earliest possible moment. I'll be returning home today. The practice is yours, so you must continue to use the surgery for the time being.'

'But I don't have to live here, too—is that what you mean?' he answered grimly. 'Don't worry—I'll leave immediately.'

He turned upon his heel and left her, and by the time she returned to Creek House, he had

122

moved out, bag and baggage, down to the village inn.

CHAPTER TEN

It didn't take Christopher long to settle in his new home. He bought the house in the centre of the village, and in a matter of weeks he was installed, using the front room as a surgery. In many ways it was convenient and suited his purpose well. Diana wasn't too pleased, however—she thought it too unostentatious, and said so.

He laughed a little at that. 'Well, no one could accuse Creek House of being exactly opulent, my dear.'

'No,' she admitted, 'but it had character and dignity. It seemed more like a doctor's house than this.'

'Well, this,' he told her, 'was the best that I could afford, and it suits my purpose well. It suits the villagers, too—they haven't so far to walk. In any case, I doubt if I could have bought Creek House even if Sally had been willing to sell it.'

'She'll be glad to sell eventually—and cheaply, at that,' Diana assured him. 'She won't be able to run it for long on the salary she's getting in that hospital job.'

Christopher frowned a little. He had been

as surprised as everyone when Sally went to work at the local hospital.

'I thought you said she was marrying Martin, and marrying him soon?'

'I certainly understood that, darling. If there's been any change of plans, I haven't heard of them. And she's obviously staying down here in order to be near him. If she wasn't going to marry him would she have taken a local job, when she could easily have returned to London? St. Mark's wanted her back.'

Diana was right, of course, and he knew it.

'Did you know she was applying for the practice?' he asked.

'I've already told you I didn't,' she answered impatiently.

She wished he would drop the subject. After all, the whole thing was settled and done with now. All that mattered was that the Executive Council had appointed him instead of Sally, and that seemed fair enough on the face of things. In fact, Diana thought that the council had done the most sensible thing, for Chris was the more experienced doctor and the people in Tresanton liked him.

Of course, they had all been sorry about Sally—some of them had even been indignant —but that feeling had quickly passed. After all, said the village folk, she was a girl, and girls married and gave up their careers, so it was far better to have a doctor who was going to stay with them and serve them for many years. Old Doctor Peterson would naturally have been disappointed, had he known, but, on the other hand, he had liked young Doctor Maynard very much and praised his medical skill. So, taken all in all, everything had perhaps happened for the best.

As for Creek House, Christopher didn't blame Sally for refusing to give it up. As he had once remarked to Diana, it was a place worth clinging to, and he would have felt the same way about it had it been his. For his own part, he was well content. He had found a place that suited him, and his initial regret at the thought of depriving Sally of the practice had passed. He believed now that it was just a sentimental gesture on her part to want the practice for a brief period. Soon she would have given it up for marriage, and he would have lost his opportunity to stay in Tresanton.

So he plunged into work, resolving to forget her. Whenever they chanced to meet, antagonism flared between them, so it was better to avoid her. There seemed no hope of ever attaining understanding, let alone friendship, with her—even had he wanted to, which he wasn't so sure about now.

The things she had said to him that memorable morning had gone deep; he couldn't forget them. If it came to that, he couldn't forget her, either, and the only possible reason for this, as far as he could see, was that she annoyed him intensely. The memory of her was an irritant which he could only forget in work, or Diana's company.

He wasn't the only one who felt this need for work. Sally felt it, too. She had to do something to assuage her sense of grief and loss. The double blow of losing her father, and then of losing the chance to carry on his work, had struck deep. Perhaps the only person who realised this was old Martha. Martin, sympathetic as he was, didn't really understand. She even felt that he was glad in a way—glad, at least, that she hadn't been appointed to the practice.

He didn't continue to pester her about marrying him, but she knew it was there in his mind all the time. Even when she took the local hospital job he seemed to raise a mental eyebrow and to smile a secret smile, as if he were regarding a child who was just playing at work and was willing to wait until the whim passed.

But old Martha understood. She had practically brought Sally up and knew her as a mother knew her own child.

'It were a shame,' she declared more than once, 'a real shame! The old Doctor would be heart-broken if he knew you weren't allowed to do what he'd planned for you.'

'Well, he doesn't know,' Sally retorted briskly one day, 'so let's not talk about it any more, Martha.'

The old woman regarded her with kind, shrewd eyes.

'Well, Miss Sally, I always think it's a good thing to talk about things—it gets them off your chest like. Much better than bottling things up inside, if I may say so. Of course . . .' and here she heaved a great sigh, 'the ideal thing would have been for you and Doctor Maynard to share the practice between you, that's what *I* say.'

Sally rounded on her hotly. 'Share a practice with *him*! Work with a man like that! I can't imagine anything I'd dislike more!'

Martha sighed again. Miss Sally seemed to be in one of her pig-headed moods, and when that happened it was no use arguing with her. She'd taken a dislike to Doctor Maynard, which was a pity. Her father had liked him all right; in fact, he liked him very much—and so do I, if it comes to that, Martha thought to herself. And I can't really blame him for applying for the practice. He deserved it, in a way. He put a lot of work into it during those six months. The mistake he made was not letting Miss Sally *know* that he was applying— it kind of cut the ground from under her feet, I expect, when she heard.

And Martha sighed again. Young people were so stupid—even the cleverest of them! There was young Doctor Maynard, as nice a young man as there ever was and a good doctor, too, and there was Miss Sally—the best

127 .

girl, in her opinion, that had ever been born in Tresanton, but as stubborn as they come. Now why couldn't two such people come together in a sensible way? But oh dear, no—Sally had taken a dislike to Christopher Maynard, and nothing would budge her from that.

The pity of it! Martha thought. A nicer young man it would really be hard to meet. She even liked him better than Mr. Penfold, although she couldn't really say why. Martin Penfold came of a highly respectable family, there was no doubt of that, and he had loved Sally for years. He was always a gentleman, too—never rude, never losing his temper, always doing the right thing in the right way at the right moment; whereas young Doctor Maynard had the devil of a temper when he chose—and he'd certainly shown it that morning when Sally burst in and accused him the way she did!

Martha had never heard Miss Sally round on anyone in such a way before. Tantrums she'd had as a small girl, normal childish tantrums, but nothing so strong and terrible as the mood she'd turned on Doctor Maynard that day. She'd hated him at that moment, and had certainly shown it.

Oh, the pity of it all! Martha thought again. Maybe it would be a good thing if Miss Sally did marry Martin Penfold, after all, although secretly, in her deep and capacious heart, Martha had always hoped for something a little more romantic than the son of a staid solicitor. As the years went by; he would grow as staid as his father, she was sure. And Sally was a girl with spirit. Wouldn't she be bored by a precise legal mind?

Really, thought Martha, I've no right to be thinking such things. If Doctor Peterson thought Mr. Penfold a suitable husband for his daughter, I'm sure he was right.

Although, of course, she knew that parents always wanted safe husbands for their daughters—someone to continue the care and protection which they themselves must ultimately relinquish. But was a quiet, protective man the sort who really made a girl happy? Although she had never married, Martha doubted it—she doubted it very much, at any rate for Miss Sally. The girl needed a man with character and strength and spirit— and the devil of a temper, too, when necessary. Someone to rule her; someone to stir her to the depths.

Martha was deep in such thoughts one afternoon when waiting for the bus home from Truro. It was market day, the queues were long and she was heavily laden. Also, her feet were aching unbearably, and it seemed like a gesture from heaven when a car pulled up beside her and a man's voice said:

'Give me those bags, Martha, and climb in beside me. I'm on my way home myself.'

It was young Doctor Maynard. Martha's

face lit up at the sight of him. She had hardly seen him since he left Creek House, but only now did she realise how much she had missed him. In the six months that he had lodged there, he had become part of the place. He'd fitted in quite naturally, as one of the family.

Her thoughts flew back to the weekend when Sally had come home and seen her father for the last time. There had been no restraint between the two young people then, no animosity, no antagonism, but now it had leapt as a barrier between them, and she knew that as long as it lasted, Christopher would never visit Creek House again.

She said: 'It's good to see you, Doctor—real good.'

'Good to see you too, Martha. I've been wondering how you were. How's that rheumatism of yours?'

She shrugged her ample shoulders. 'Oh, just about the same. I just gets on with me work and takes no notice of it. Or tries to.'

'Are you still taking those pills I prescribed?'

Her broad, amiable face broke into a grin. 'When I remember, Doctor. Although I must admit it's Miss Sally that does the remembering for me. Chases me after every meal, she does, with a box in her hands.'

'And a good thing, too,' said Christopher, his voice impersonal.

So he's not going to ask how Miss Sally is, Martha thought. Why, I wonder? Because he's not interested—or because the poor man's too embarrassed?

She suppressed a sigh, eased her broad country shoes off her swollen feet, and said with relief

'My, that's better! That market place was hard to walk on today.'

'You shouldn't do it,' he said severely. 'I've told you more than once not to carry such heavy loads. Miss Peterson shouldn't allow it.'

Oh, so it's 'Miss Peterson', is it? Martha thought with secret amusement. Didn't he like to mention her Christian name, then? And if not, why not?

'You mustn't blame Miss Sally, Doctor. She's always on to me about it. So when I decide to come to market, I just don't tell her—that's all! It's the easiest way. So you'll oblige me, sir,' she added, 'by not telling her yourself.'

He wasn't likely to have the opportunity, he thought wryly. He never saw Sally these days, except when she drove past his house on the way to work. Her job at the local hospital was a non-resident one, enabling her to live at home, which meant that she drove to work each day in her father's ancient car. Her route took her through the centre of the village past Christopher's house, but this she studiously ignored, and if a greeting between them was unavoidable, it was distant, but courteous, on both sides.

131

Nevertheless, Christopher had found himself watching for her passing on more than one occasion; in fact, it seemed to be becoming a habit—an easy one, since his windows faced directly on to the street, and he was more than familiar with the sound of George Peterson's old car. He had driven it himself often enough about these country roads and so, automatically, as it came rattling down the village street, he would glance from his window—and wonder why he did so.

'And how is Miss Peterson?' he asked stiffly, not because he wanted to, but because in the circumstances it was unavoidable. Besides, somehow or other she had crept into the conversation. That was natural enough, of course. Martha lived for the girl, and well he knew it.

'Oh, she's fine,' Martha assured him. 'Doing very well in that job of hers.'

'So I hear,' he admitted.

In medical circles these things got around, and the hardworking young house-physician at the local hospital was talked about and praised quite a bit.

'Well, it's not surprising, is it, sir, seeing as how she's her father's daughter?'

No, he thought, it wasn't surprising. Sally was a good doctor—several of his own patients had told him so on being discharged from hospital. He was genuinely glad that she was doing so well. In the course of his work,

Christopher had come in frequent touch with the chief physician at the hospital and others on the staff—all of whom spoke highly of her.

He steered the conversation into less personal channels until they reached the gates of Creek House, and it wasn't until he was half-way up the drive that he saw Sally's car parked there.

Martha saw it, too, and her face fell.

'Oh dear,' she said, 'now I'm for it! I wasn't expecting Miss Sally to get home before me. Maybe I can slip in through the back door and she won't know where I've been.'

And maybe I can slip away, thought Christopher hopefully. A meeting on the very doorstep of her home would be more than embarrassing!

But his luck was out—and Martha's, too—for at that moment the front door opened and Sally appeared. She stood upon the doorstep, briefly eyeing Martha's heavy shopping bags, and then marched towards her saying sternly:

'How many times have I told you not to go to the market, Martha?'

'Now, none of that please, Miss Sally! There's no sense in paying more for things in the shops when you can go to the market and get 'em cheap.'

'And there's no sense in killing yourself, either,' Sally retorted briskly. 'If you must go to the market, we can drive there together on Saturdays when I'm not on duty.'

She pulled up abruptly, seeing Christopher for the first time. A deep flush mounted her cheeks—a flush of anger, he thought. And he wasn't far wrong.

How *dare* he come here? she thought furiously.

Martha's voice said calmly: 'The Doctor brought me all the way back from Truro. Wasn't that kind, now?'

'Very kind,' Sally agreed stiffly. 'Thank you, Christopher.'

Well, thought Martha with satisfaction, she's not adverse to using *his* Christian name, despite her high and mighty manner towards him.

The old woman ambled comfortably towards the kitchen door, saying over her shoulder: 'I'll have tea ready in less than five minutes. You'll stay and have a cup, won't you, sir?'

'I don't think I . . .' Christopher began, then realised that his protest was wasted, for Sally, too, was disappearing towards the house, saying: 'Tea's ready, Martha, so you needn't bother. All we'll need is an extra cup for the Doctor.'

He thought to himself furiously: I don't want her blasted cup of tea! I don't want to sit opposite her, looking at her frigid young face, knowing all the time that she resents and even hates me! But he was given no choice. She was being polite to him, at least, and he had to be

134

the same. So he followed her indoors.

The moment he stepped across the threshold into the cool, white-panelled hall, he had a sense of home-coming. He stood for a moment looking about him, as if greeting the place after a long absence. He realised with a sense of shock that it was barely a few weeks since he had left here. It seemed more like an eternity.

Before Martha brought the tea tray from the kitchen, he was alone with Sally briefly. She offered him a cigarette and made polite conversation, inquiring in an impersonal way, which suggested that she had no real interest, whether he had settled down comfortably in his new home.

'Very comfortably, thank you.'

'I've always thought it rather an attractive place,' she admitted.

Christopher was surprised to hear himself reply: 'Then you must come and visit it some time. I hope the inside will match up to your expectations.'

'Oh, it does,' she assured him. 'I know the house well. The previous owner was a patient of my father's.'

He had blundered badly, and he knew it, but since everyone in Tresanton had been a patient of her father's at some time or another, that was hardly to be avoided.

Martha bustled in with the tea tray, her tired feet forgotten in the pleasure of having young Doctor Maynard back in the house—a pleasure so undisguised that Sally wanted to shake her. She knew perfectly well how highly Martha regarded him, for she had had the fact rammed down her throat often enough.

'Well now, sir, isn't it lucky,' Martha beamed, 'I made some of your favourite gingerbread only this morning!'

Sally's fury increased, and in the private corners of her mind she made a resolution to tell Martha afterwards precisely what she thought of her for buttering up this man the way she was doing. What was it about young Doctor Maynard that endeared him to more than half the inhabitants of Tresanton? Wherever I go, I hear his praises sung, Sally thought furiously, and I'm getting heartily sick of it!

She cut Martha's gingerbread unseeingly, remarking icily: 'You're specially favoured, Doctor. Martha only brings out her gingerbread for guests of honour.' She laid particular emphasis upon the final word—an emphasis which quivered between them as sharply as an arrow thrust.

Anger struck warning little chords in his mind, but he managed to control them sufficiently to reply: 'Then I must make the most of it. I always did make the most of your home-made cakes, didn't I, Martha?'

They're as bad as each other, Sally reflected bitterly, each emphasising their fondness for one another—as if he were still part of the household.

Martha hovered about them with motherly concern. 'You're not eating anything, Miss Sally,' she reproached.

'I'm not hungry, Martha.'

The old woman regarded her as anxiously as a mother hen surveying a troublesome chick. There must be something the matter with Sally, she thought. Usually, when she gets back from the hospital, she's simply ravenous; and no wonder—she works hard enough from all accounts. Too hard, I'm thinking, for Mr. Penfold's liking.

As if some mental telepathy had conjured up his name, Sally said: 'I'm dining with Martin tonight, so don't prepare anything for me, will you, Martha?'

The housekeeper clucked with annoyance. 'Well now, miss, I wish I'd known that! I left supper all prepared before I went to market— steak and kidney pie, too, what you're so fond of.'

'I'm quite sure Doctor Maynard would be only too pleased to stay and eat it with you.'

'Well now, that's a nice idea!' the old woman agreed. 'What about it, sir?' and a smile which was almost conspiratorial flickered across her homely face.

As if taking his cue from her, Christopher answered easily: 'Thank you, Martha, that *is* a very nice idea. I think I'll take you up on it.'

Sally finished her tea, laid down her cup, and rose. 'If you'll excuse me,' she said, 'I must go upstairs and change. Martin will be here soon.'

So the fellow was still around, Christopher thought as she left the room. Well, was it so very surprising? Didn't he expect him to be?

When Sally had gone upstairs and Martha was busily carrying away the tea things, Christopher said: 'I'll help you wash up,' and, picking up the tray, he carried it out to the kitchen.

'There's no need for that, sir, I'm sure you've got much better things to do.'

Christopher stacked the dishes in the sink, turned on the hot-water tap, and smiled at her over his shoulder. 'What could be better than this?' he said. 'It's like old times, isn't it, Martha?'

'Well, almost, sir,' she admitted sadly. 'As near like old times as it can be without the old doctor. And, of course, Miss Sally's changed, in a way.'

'In what way?' he asked bluntly.

Martha picked up a tea towel and began to dry a cup thoughtfully. 'It's a little difficult to say, really. On the surface she's still the same, I suppose still kind, still thoughtful.'

That wasn't how he remembered her—not, at any rate, at their last meeting—and as if sensing his thoughts, Martha said: 'Oh, I know she gave you the sharp edge of her tongue, sir,

138

but you mustn't hold that against her—not in the circumstances, if I may say so.'

But he did hold it against her. Her accusations had been grossly unjust. He said: 'Do you think, if I'd known that she was going to apply for the practice, I would have done so, too, Martha?'

'I don't see why you both shouldn't have it, sir,' she answered simply.

Christopher finished washing the tea things. He dried his hands upon a roller towel on the back of the kitchen door, and then took hold of Martha's shoulders, looking down into her face affectionately.

'That wasn't possible,' he said gently.

'I don't see why not! She was coming home to be her father's assistant. Well, why couldn't she have been yours, instead?'

He laughed aloud.

'I can just see her agreeing to be *my* assistant! Oh, no, Martha, it just wouldn't have worked. I'm sorry she was disappointed, but I'm not sorry I applied for the practice—nor that I got it. After all, she wouldn't have stayed in it for very long.'

Martha's honest old eyes regarded him with surprise. 'Now why d'you say that, sir? What gives you such an idea?'

'Simply because when she married she'd give up working as a doctor.'

'Oh no, sir, I'm sure she'd never do that! Many's the time I've heard her say that

139

doctoring is as much a woman's job as a man's, and that so long as she didn't neglect her family, a woman could continue in it after she was married.'

'Providing,' he pointed out, 'that her husband was agreeable.'

'Well, Miss Sally hasn't got a husband.'

'But she soon will have.'

'Soon? It's the first I've heard of it.'

'But you knew she was going to marry Martin Penfold, surely?'

Martha made a gesture with which he was very familiar—a deep shrug of her wide shoulders; a doubtful, sceptical gesture.

'Well now, sir, there's always been some as have predicted that, but it hasn't happened yet, has it?'

So Sally had certainly kept the old woman in the dark, he thought. In that case it was not for him to say anything further.

'Well, I'll be getting along, Martha. Thanks for the tea, and if I can take you up on that supper invitation, I'll be back.'

He saw a worried little crease between her brows.

'Wait a moment, sir, please! What you said just now about Miss Sally only going to handle her father's practice until she married, and then giving it all up . . .'

'Well?' he queried gently.

'What makes you think that, sir? Did you believe it when you sent in your application?

Was that why you did?'

'Of course, Martha.'

'But what *made* you think it, sir?'

He found it impossible to tell her that Diana had been responsible for the information. If Martin had confided the news to Diana in confidence, then it was not for him to spread it any further.

So he answered evasively: 'Sally's father told me that she would marry Martin eventually.'

'Lots of things are taken for granted, if I may say so, that never come true.'

The words startled him—the more so because they came from Martha, who knew Sally so well, who had brought her up from babyhood, who knew of her father's plans and dreams—and of Sally's too, no doubt.

A sudden uneasiness crept into his mind, and in the hope of assuaging it he said:

'But she's staying in Tresanton for Martin's sake, isn't she?'

'Lots of people in the village seem to think so,' Martha agreed, 'but there could be another reason, Doctor.'

'And that?' he asked.

'Why, simply that she wanted to come home. She's always wanted to come home—I know that. She used to say so in her letters from that hospital in London. She loves this house, and she loves this place—and where a person's heart is, that's where they stay, sir.'

He knew very well how true that was.

141

Hadn't it been his own reason for remaining? But it wasn't Sally's—he was convinced of that, for he knew how inseparable she and Martin were. The young solicitor had been her constant companion since her return, and a possessive one, too. Christopher had seen them together frequently, and Martin's proprietary air never escaped him. It confirmed all that Diana had told him, and, unless Sally were willing, would she allow herself to be so monopolised?

This conviction was confirmed when he came face to face with Martin in the hall. Sally was running downstairs—looking very attractive, Christopher observed in a detached corner of his mind. She wore a simple grey dress which exactly matched the colour of her eyes, and she looked very charming in it. At the foot of the stairs Martin met her, took hold of both her hands and surveyed her with frank appreciation. Then he put his arms about her and kissed her.

Sally accepted the kiss, as always, with a passive sort of pleasure, and then, glancing up, saw Christopher surveying them. Promptly, she slipped both her arms about Martin's neck and kissed him full upon the lips.

Martin was distinctly gratified—even more so because this unexpected demonstration had been witnessed by someone else—but he was surprised to see Christopher. Nevertheless, he held out his hand and greeted him amiably.

Christopher shook hands with him, and said: 'How are you, Penfold? I haven't seen you for quite a time.'

'Oh, fine, fine,' Martin assured him. 'And don't you think Sally's looking well these days?'

'Extremely well,' Christopher agreed.

'That's because I'm around to keep an eye on her,' Martin said complacently—and managed to convey a subtle suggestion that the occupation would shortly be a permanent one.

Christopher said good-bye, thanked Sally for the tea, and went on his way. But he hadn't enjoyed himself much, apart from that little interval in the kitchen with dear old Martha. In fact, in an inexplicable sort of way he felt irritated, and if that was the effect Sally Peterson had upon him he hoped he wouldn't meet her again for a very long time.

CHAPTER ELEVEN

If Sally had felt the need for work following her disappointment over the practice, she felt it even more after this last meeting with Christopher. She couldn't understand why, but it was there—a deep and urgent need to plunge herself into work.

Since there is no place on earth so busy as a hospital, she was able to do this. Compared with the vast East End hospital where she had worked and trained, the local one was a small affair, consisting only of Medical and Surgical wards, Casualty and Out-Patients Departments, a Children's Wing, and a small Therapeutic Block built in the grounds; but it had the personal and intimate air exclusive to many small hospitals.

Sally had felt immediately at home there. The Matron had been an old friend of her father's, and remembered him from the days when he had been a Senior House-Physician at the time she herself was a third-year nurse. Her welcome to Sally had been sincere, and so, too, the welcome extended by the rest of the medical staff—all of whom had known and respected George Peterson.

So Sally had not been plunged into a new and alien atmosphere, and although she had been tempted to rush straight back to St. Mark's in the first fury of her indignation, she was soon glad that she had yielded to an impulse to remain in the vicinity.

Why should I run away, she had thought angrily, just because Christopher Maynard has dethroned me? I'll stay right here under his nose, and hold my head up proudly!

She knew that everyone was surprised at her taking this house-physician's job. They had all fully expected her to do one of two things— either to marry Martin, or go back to London. By now everyone knew that St. Mark's had wanted her back. The kindlier inhabitants of the village assumed that she had preferred to stay in order to be near Martin, and that their wedding would not be so very far off, after all—and if Martin himself put that interpretation upon things, Sally couldn't stop him. Besides, it was easier somehow—easier than making excuses and evasions, all of which seemed more and more necessary as the weeks went by.

There was plenty of work for her to do at the hospital, and she threw herself into it wholeheartedly.

The day after Christopher's unexpected visit to Creek House, Sally was on duty in Out-Patients. She was glad of this for two reasons—first, because that department was always extremely busy and gave her no chance to relax, and, second, because it brought her into contact with many of the village people whom she knew. They were all Christopher's patients now, of course, but at one time they had been her father's, and for this reason, if for no other, her interest in them was deeply personal. Besides, she was a doctor herself, a doctor in mind and heart and thought, and the work absorbed her utterly.

This was something, she knew, that Martin would never understand, and the thought had troubled her more and more since her return—for if a man and a woman intended to marry, surely a mutual interest in each other's

145

work was important? But Martin had no interest at all in medicine, and indeed saw no reason why he should have—but he did expect her to take an interest in his legal cases. A wife should always interest herself in her husband's work, he said—which seemed somehow a little unfair, to Sally's way of thinking, if he was not prepared to reciprocate that interest.

But all such thoughts and anxieties were driven from her mind that afternoon by the long line of patients awaiting her attention— some for post-operative check-ups and some for new examinations and courses of treatment. Quite a few were patients of Christopher's, and Sally experienced a strange and indefinable reaction when reading the notes they brought along, all written in his characteristic handwriting—all brief, professional and to the point. Nothing could be more impersonal than a note from one doctor to another, and it was therefore quite unreasonable to react as she did.

But one other thing struck her, and that was the deep and implicit trust his patients had in him.

'Doctor Maynard said I should come along,' they would say. 'He thinks a course of infra-red would be good for me,'—obviously implying that if he said so, no further examination or report was necessary, whereupon Sally would be left to explain that the system in this small hospital was different from that in many larger ones. Before visiting Physiotherapy or X-ray Departments, patients had to pass through Out-Patients as a matter of routine, and thus it was that several of Christopher's patients in need of hospital treatment came her way—and again, inexplicably, she would feel a quickening of interest in their cases, which she stubbornly attributed to the fact that they had been all on her father's list previously.

But the young woman who came in at about four o'clock had not. She was a newcomer to Tresanton—a Devonshire girl who had married one of the workers at the chalk pits, and come to the village as his bride only a year ago. She was now expecting her first baby and things were not going quite normally. She was young, and a little frightened at the idea of being X-rayed. She sat a little tensely on the edge of her chair, her pretty young face pale and anxious. She was as fragile and diminutive as a doll—not the sturdy young countrywoman one expected from an agricultural county.

Sally took an interest in her at once, and as at that precise moment the duty nurse brought in a cup of tea for her, ordered one for the girl as well. Within five minutes Sally had the satisfaction of seeing the tenseness and fear vanish.

Over tea, Sally chatted in a friendly and non-professional manner, asking the girl how she liked living in Cornwall, and what kind of a job her husband did at Langdon's Chalk Mills. She was gratified by the girl's declaration that she never wanted to live anywhere in the world but Tresanton.

'We've got one of the new cottages, just outside the village,' she said with pride.

'One of those Mr. Langdon built for the workers?' Sally asked with interest.

'Yes, Miss . . . er, Doctor, I mean,' the girl corrected hastily, thinking to herself how odd it was to be calling a girl so young as this 'Doctor', It didn't seem right, somehow. She'd heard of Doctor Peterson's daughter, of course—who hadn't? But she looked awfully young in that white overall—and there she was, talking just like one girl to another. Still, she was nice—awfully nice. She had a quick bright smile, and no side about her at all—nothing to frighten anyone.

The girl's last flickering doubt and anxiety disappeared. It was the first time that she'd ever stepped inside a hospital and the very atmosphere had frightened her.

Whilst the girl finished her tea, Sally picked up Christopher's letter and re-read it. The patient's name was Stella Blundell, aged twenty-two, and she was six months pregnant. All had gone well, apparently, until this last week, when the position of the child had changed and was now likely to cause complications which an X-ray would confirm. There was no cause for anxiety, however, unless a premature birth occurred.

She heard the girl's voice saying: 'Doctor Maynard said I wasn't to worry.'

'He was quite right,' Sally agreed. 'Worrying never helped anyone, you know.'

Stella Blundell laid aside her teacup. 'The funny thing is that I don't worry when I see Doctor Maynard. He's so reassuring, and understanding—if you know what I mean.'

'I know what you mean,' Sally said quietly.

'But it's afterwards, when I get home, or when Jim's on night shift and I'm all alone, that I begin to feel . . . well, I've never had a baby before, you see. Jim tells me I couldn't be in better hands than Doctor Maynard's. He's wonderful, isn't he?' She giggled a little. 'Doctor Maynard, I mean, of course!'

Sally smiled and politely agreed.

'The results of the X-ray will go straight to Doctor Maynard,' she told the girl. 'He'll let you know when he hears.'

She wrote the necessary note for the girl to take downstairs, rang for the nurse, and said good-bye to Stella.

'I hope I see you again, Mrs. Blundell—but not here, of course. I'll look out for you when I pass your house. I drive by every morning on my way to hospital, you know.'

The girl smiled and departed with the nurse. Sally watched her go, and was aware of a surprising envy—a feeling she had never really known before; an illogical envy, since she

149

herself had so much more than the girl—
materially, at least. She had a job which she
enjoyed doing, work which interested her, and
the home that she had always loved so much.
She was finding it a bit of a strain financially to
maintain Creek House—at any rate on her
present salary—but she wasn't doing too badly,
and Martha was a wonderful housekeeper.

She had Martin, too, and if she married him
she would have no cause to envy little Stella.
She could have children of her own—but did
she want Martin to be their father? The
question was an important one—so important
that she turned back to her work abruptly,
telling herself that this was neither the time
nor place to think of such things, but knowing
in her heart that she was simply refusing to
face the issue, and that the sooner she decided
one way or another about him, the better it
would be.

But the question of breaking with Martin
altogether was one she simply couldn't
contemplate. She had come to rely upon him
more and more, both for help and advice,
since her father's death. He was the best friend
she had, but that, she thought honestly, was
the root of the matter—that it was as a friend
that she really wanted him.

She rang briskly for the next patient and
resolutely thought of nothing but work for the
rest of the afternoon.

It was growing dusk when she left the

hospital. The nights were beginning to draw in and there was a nip of autumn in the air. The hedges, she noticed as she drove home, were laden with berries—a particularly heavy crop this year, and a sure sign, said the country people, of a hard winter to come. Leaves were beginning to fall and swirled ahead of her upon the road in little golden clouds. There was the smell of wood smoke in the air—a sign that gardens were being tidied up at the end of the season.

Passing the row of cottages where young Mrs. Blundell lived, Sally's glance turned automatically towards number five. There was a strapping young man, in his shirt sleeves, busily raking up leaves from the small area of front garden, and at that precise moment his wife opened the door and called to him. Sally braked automatically and, seeing her, the girl came shyly down the garden path.

'I hope you didn't have to wait long down in X-ray?' Sally said. 'It wasn't much of an ordeal, was it?'

'Oh no, Doctor, thank you. It didn't hurt a bit.'

Sally laughed spontaneously. 'Surely you didn't expect it to?'

'Well, I didn't know what to expect. I've never been X-rayed before.'

The girl turned and, glancing towards her husband, said shyly: 'This is Jim,' and the young man came forward, wiping his hands

151

apologetically upon the seat of his trousers.

They were a nice young couple, clean and wholesome and obviously very much in love. Sally's glance passed from them to the neat little semi-detached cottage, and then around the pretty little garden.

'You've made great strides in only a year,' she said.

Jim Blundell laughed. 'Well, there isn't much labour to a patch this size, Doctor.'

'Oh, but we've a nice piece at the back, as well,' Stella put in proudly. 'Would you like to see it?'

And the next thing Sally knew, she was being shown more than the garden—the house itself, neat and shining and clean as a new pin. She saw everything from the bright little kitchen to the small room which Stella was preparing for the coming child. There was a simplicity about this couple which appealed to Sally, and she found she was enjoying the visit tremendously—even the cup of strong tea which Stella pressed upon her before departing. Sally didn't really want it. She was on her way home to one of Martha's good meals, but she couldn't hurt the girl by refusing, and it was obvious that they enjoyed sharing their tea with her.

She was laying her cup aside and preparing to depart, when Jim, slipping his arm about his wife's shoulder, said to Sally anxiously: 'She *is* going to be all right, isn't she, Miss . . . I mean,

Doctor?' He laughed a little apologetically, and added: 'I'm sorry, but everyone in Tresanton still thinks of you as Miss Sally. It's hard to get used to the idea of your being Doctor Peterson now.'

Sally pulled on her gloves and said: 'I've actually been Doctor Peterson for quite a time, Jim, but so long as people don't forget I'm a doctor, I don't mind in the least if they still think of me as Miss Sally.'

They came with her into the tiny hall, but before Jim Blundell opened the front door, Sally said again: 'And don't worry about your wife. Of course she's going to be all right. Doctor Maynard will tell you as soon as he hears the result of the X-ray. That's only a precaution, you know—and a useful one. It simply tells us what to look out for. But in any case, there's plenty of time for Nature herself to take a hand. There are three more months before the baby is due, and by that time everything may be quite normal. And,' she finished, 'Stella is in the hands of a very good doctor.'

The young man's relief showed itself on his honest face. 'It was nice of you to stop by,' he said. 'I hope you'll do so again, Doctor.'

It was perhaps unfortunate that Christopher Maynard should call at that precise moment, just when they were all talking amiably together on the other side of the front door. Jim reached out and opened it automatically when the bell rang, and for a brief moment they stood there like statues in a tableau, with Christopher looking at them from the outside.

He was surprised to see Sally—that much was obvious—and she felt a flush of embarrassment and guilt. It would seem odd to him, to say the least, to find her visiting his patient.

Well, she thought defiantly, he'll just have to put whatever interpretation upon it that he wishes! And she held out her hand and said good-bye to Stella.

'It was nice of you to call, Doctor Peterson,' the girl said, unwittingly making matters worse.

Christopher was talking to Jim Blundell, making the excuse that he had called to ascertain whether his wife had attended at the hospital for her X-ray, but hiding his real reason—which had been purely and simply because he had seen Sally's car standing at the gate. The sight of it had surprised him, and the swift suspicion that she was paying an unethical visit on one of his patients darted into his mind. He had been ashamed of the thought immediately, but, nevertheless, there seemed no reason for such a visit.

Sally knew what he was thinking. It was inevitable and excusable. She felt embarrassed and anxious to put things right, so she said: 'Mrs. Blundell's been showing me her house. It's absolutely charming.' She turned to the young wife and said again: 'Thank you for letting me see it.'

She said good night pleasantly to them all and departed, hoping that she had eased the moment. It was the most she could do. She was not prepared to wait for Christopher and make an embarrassed apology, and if, after her last remark, he still doubted her real reason for being there, then he would simply have to get on with it, she thought impatiently.

CHAPTER TWELVE

Sally returned to Creek House to find Diana awaiting her. It was a matter of weeks since the two girls had met and Diana had come to repair the omission. 'Do you *live* for that hospital?' she chaffed good-naturedly. 'Or haven't you time for your old friends any more?'

The accusation was unjust, and she knew it, but it was also defensive. She felt guilty for her neglect of Sally, whom she had given a wide berth since Christopher stepped into Doctor Peterson's practice. But there had been no repercussions, no awkward situations, and she was quite sure that Sally herself didn't suspect how large a part she had played in persuading Chris to apply for it. And now, surely, the whole episode had died down and life could go

155

on as before? Sally had settled in a new job, and happily from all accounts, so there was no reason on earth why their friendship should not be resumed.

Besides, it would be wise to pick up the threads again, as well as being desirable and pleasant. In this small social world they were bound to bump into each other, and to re-establish their old friendly footing would make things easier all round. And if she kept Sally under her eye she would know how often she and Christopher met, and what their attitude towards each other now was.

For Christopher never referred to Sally these days. That could be a good sign, or a bad one, indicating that he was either indifferent to her, or too much aware of her to wish to discuss her. So it was about time, thought Diana shrewdly, that they teamed up as before . . . herself and Chris; Sally and Martin.

'I've missed you, Sally,' she said reproachfully.

Sally couldn't honestly say the same. Her job at the hospital occupied her too actively, and her spare time was spent mainly with Martin. So she side-stepped that remark, commenting lightly that Diana was looking as lovely as ever. 'And that's a very nice suit you're wearing. You didn't buy *that* in Tresanton!'

'A little woman in Falmouth, my dear. I must introduce you to her. She trained in

Mayfair, and now she's come back to Cornwall and opened her own little *couturiére* place ...'

'At Mayfair prices?' Sally laughed. 'If so, she's not for me, and you know it, Diana.'

'Well, darling, to get anything decent these days one must pay a decent price. It's false economy not to. And with your figure you *could* look wonderful ...'

Sally chuckled. That remark was so typical of Diana that she let it pass.

'I'm a mere house-physician, Diana. Have you any idea what kind of a salary that job commands? Not enough to run to Creek House *and* exclusive little dressmakers ...'

'Well, I think you're crazy to even try to maintain this house. Why do you, Sally? It's far too big, just for you and old Martha ...'

Sally's young mouth closed stubbornly. She wasn't going to reveal her ambitions any more than she was going to reveal her heart. Her dreams were locked away with her emotions, and sternly guarded. Only Martha, perhaps, knew how she felt about her home, how she could never tear up her roots or put the place up for sale. How she loved it, and worked for it, and dreamed of the day when a brass plate would once more adorn the wrought-iron gate, bearing the name of Doctor S. Peterson, M.D.

It was only a matter of patience, of biding her time, of working hard and getting experience, until a hardened Executive Council judged her sufficiently qualified to re-establish

157

a surgery at Creek House. That they might still refuse, on the grounds that Tresanton was adequately served by Doctor Maynard in the village, was possible, of course, but she refused to think of that. Tresanton was a growing community—and hope was a commodity of which Sally had plenty.

Martha thrust her head round the door and beamed maternally.

'I thought I heard you come in, Miss Sally. You're late home this evening . . .'

'I stopped to visit a patient.'

Diana's attention sharpened.

'You've no right to do that, have you? All patients in Tresanton are Christopher's now.'

'I know. This was one of his, too, but I wasn't visiting her professionally. She came as an Out-Patient for an X-ray today, and I happened to see her as I passed her cottage. She wouldn't let me go by without meeting her husband. He's one of your father's employees, Diana—Jim Blundell. A nice young man.'

Diana shrugged indifferently. She wasn't interested in the pit workers.

Martha was fidgeting.

'You're supper's keeping hot, Miss Sally. It will spoil if it's left too long.'

'That,' drawled Diana, 'is a hint for me to go.' She strolled towards the door, saying over her shoulder:

'I only dropped in to see if you were free tomorrow evening. If so, come along for

158

cocktails at six, Sally. It seems ages since we had a good natter together. I'm dying to hear about your job at the hospital—and all your news.'

'I haven't any, Diana, but I'd like to come, just the same.' Sally felt an amused indulgence towards her friend, knowing perfectly well that hospital talk would undoubtedly bore her.

'Bring Martin with you,' Diana said casually as she departed. 'Chris will be coming along, too, and we can all go on to dine somewhere. A foursome will be nice.'

So it would, too. Sally knew that, even though her first instinct was to retract. Then common sense took over. If she had to live in the same neighbourhood as Christopher Maynard she might as well do so amicably. Nursing grievances never did anyone any good, and since she and Chris were likely to meet professionally it was even greater stupidity to bear him a grudge. So she agreed with Diana wholeheartedly and was aware of a sense of gladness coupled with a sense of anticipation.

'Till tomorrow evening, then!'

Diana waved an elegantly gloved hand, and departed. She, too, felt satisfied and happy, for the meeting had gone off easily, with no restraint or embarrassment. But why should there be? she thought as she drove towards The Towers. It was Sally's attitude, not mine, which made that business over the practice so

159

unpleasant. But it's over now. All over. Chris is the man in possession and a girl like Sally isn't likely to oust him out. *And* she knows it. She's obviously happy at the hospital, too, which proves that she only wanted to dabble in medicine until she married, so I've nothing on my conscience. Nothing at all!

Not that Diana's conscience was either tender or retentive. It had a glossy veneer which rendered it impervious to more than superficial damage. Guilt or shame could slide from its surface like water from a duck's feathers and she didn't even have to shake it to dislodge the drops. Besides, what had she to feel guilty about? She had told Christopher nothing but the truth concerning Martin and Sally. They *were* going to marry sooner or later—everyone knew that. And if Martin had his way it would be sooner rather than later . . .

So why wasn't he getting his way? And why did Sally cling to that old house—that lovely, gracious old house which Diana herself rather fancied—instead of shaking the dust from her feet, pocketing the proceeds, and thereby ridding herself of a lot of responsibility and worry? As she herself said, a house-physician's job carried a poor salary—especially in a small country hospital. Then why did she *take* the job, when Martin was ready and waiting to marry her, to free her of all responsibility and financial anxiety? It just didn't make sense.

And if it didn't make sense to her, Diana,

160

then the possibility was that it didn't make sense to Christopher, either.

Well, at least, thought Diana philosophically, if we all get together again I can keep my eye on both of them. I will at least see how they react to one another.

She knew the most revealing moment would be the one when Christopher and Sally came face to face with each other. If they were studiously polite she would know that a feeling of restraint existed between them, and that would be pleasing because they were both reserved people, both unlikely to make the first move to overcome such restraint. If they were self-conscious in each other's presence, that would be equally pleasing because they would obviously shun each other and she, Diana, could weigh in and annex Christopher for herself. He would willingly team up with her, in that event, and Martin—Martin, the good old standby, who knew Sally so well and with whom she felt so completely at ease— would naturally partner her. They would make a nice foursome and, once established, such an arrangement would be difficult to break up— she would see to that.

And Christopher would see for himself that what she had predicted about Sally and Martin was certainly likely to come true, so he would stop asking questions, wouldn't he? Awkward questions about whether it were really true that Sally Peterson and Martin Penfold were to marry . . .

Diana took great pains with her toilet the following evening, and was satisfied with the result. She observed that Sally had obviously come straight from the hospital, for she wore the neat little navy-blue suit with which everyone in Tresanton was more than familiar. Not that she didn't look nice in it, of course, in an unspectacular fashion. Diana's long fingers smoothed the silk jersey of her own model dress with complacent satisfaction, aware that it clung to her lovely figure in all the right places and that Christopher's eyes had already observed it admiringly.

He had been standing in the wide hall as she descended the marble staircase. Half-way down, she had called his name softly, and waited as he turned and looked up at her—waited in the curve of the stairs, at the precise spot where an elegant woman could be displayed to advantage—one hand upon the marble balustrade, the other held out to him in welcome; one foot poised above the step below, ready to descend lightly and eagerly. This was how he had seen her, and she knew that her loveliness made his breath catch. With a little laugh she ran to meet him, holding out both her hands, saying eagerly: 'Darling, how lovely of you to come early! Now we can have five minutes alone before the others arrive . . .'

If he was disappointed that the meeting was not to be *à deux* he didn't reveal it. Perhaps he

162

was too busy admiring her to heed the reference to others. Certainly he took both her hands and stood looking down at her with pleasure. 'You're lovely, Diana—lovely!' He said it with all the sincerity of a man who genuinely admired a beautiful woman, and all the warmth of a man looking upon the one he loved . . .

She didn't imagine it. She knew that Christopher had been more than half in love with her for a very long time. When she was ready, she would push him gently the rest of the way, and he would never even suspect that she had done so.

When she was ready? She was ready now, wasn't she? First, she had ensured that he remained in Tresanton by applying for Doctor Peterson's practice, and, second, she had made sure that any fleeting attraction he had felt for Sally was put in its place by announcing that her marriage to Martin Penfold was not only certain, but imminent. Both ruses had succeeded. The only thing that had gone awry was the acquisition of Creek House, on which she had set her heart. If she married him—as she now firmly intended—that mediocre house he had bought in the village wouldn't do at all. But there was still no reason why all her plans shouldn't go through. It wouldn't be long before the struggle to maintain Creek House became too much for Sally, and if her idea was to continue living in it after marrying Martin,

163

well, that idea could easily be discouraged. She could go to work on Martin for that. As a child she had always obtained the toys she wanted. Creek House, to her, was just another.

So she slipped her arm confidently through Christopher's and turned with him towards the long drawing-room. 'Daddy's out,' she said happily. 'Some dull business dinner in Falmouth—men only, thank goodness, or you may be sure I'd've been dragged there! As it is, we can enjoy ourselves . . .'

She hovered expertly over the cocktail tray, mixing a Manhattan—his favourite—and mixing it precisely as he liked it.

'So I thought,' she continued happily, 'we'd go on to dine somewhere. There's a new hotel at St. Mawes which sounds pretty good. We'll go in my car, and you can drive . . .'

She thought that would please him. He enjoyed driving powerful cars, and after that old bone-shaker of his it would be a treat for him to drive something really good. A foretaste of things to come, she thought complacently—because, of course, after they married there would be no dilapidated old cars in their lives any more than there would be mediocre village houses.

'Who else is coming?' he asked, side-stepping the reference to her car, which made him feel like a dog being thrown a particularly delectable tit-bit. Sometimes Diana's remarks had that effect upon him—he didn't know why.

Perhaps he was unduly sensitive about his own poverty—for poverty it was, compared with her wealth. A village doctor, he thought, that is all I am. A country G.P. A plodding, unambitious type with no yearning for Harley Street. At least, that is how her father sees me. That is why he is against our marriage. But if I were to toe the line, if I were to bend the knee to the great Langdon patronage and reveal a latent ambition to become a Society doctor, what a very different story it would be! Out would pour the Langdon largesse. I'd be taken in hand and launched. I'd be wearing pin-stripe trousers and a black jacket quicker than I could discard my old tweed suit, and I'd be sharing elegant consulting rooms in London with half a dozen other socially ambitious medical men, and outside a luxurious car (purchased with Langdon money) would jostle for parking space with hundreds of others . . . and I would never see Tresanton again.

Never call my soul my own again, either.

So which was it to be? Success and Diana—or his own plans and dreams? He knew he couldn't have both. But when he looked at her shining head and lovely smile, he knew he wanted both. She was very feminine, very desirable, and she was the only woman he knew who had the power to stir him deeply and passionately. Physically, he wanted her very much, and his desire was increasing—especially since he left Creek House. Alone in his village home he would think of her with longing, wishing she were there to come back to from his rounds, and if the cause of such desire was mainly one of loneliness, that didn't make it any the less potent or disturbing.

But somehow he could never really visualise her in his new village home. Creek House, yes, for in the old days, when he had worked as Doctor Peterson's locum, she had visited them frequently, and loved the place as much as he. That always surprised him, until he learned what a simple girl she was at heart and that despite her father's wealth she disliked ostentation and display. That was why she was unhappy at The Towers. 'Creek House is *my* type of place,' she had said once, wistfully. 'That is why I feel at home there, Christopher.'

He had even indulged a dream in which she had rejected her father's wealth for marriage with himself—and life as a country G.P.'s wife. It had been so easy to dream, as long as he lived in Creek House, for it was easy to picture her against such a background. He had seen her there a hundred times. The place had grace and dignity and a certain shabby elegance. It stood proudly in its own superb setting beside the curving bay. It was small, but spacious. It had character and charm and beauty. In fact, it was a very different home altogether from the plain terraced Victorian house in the centre of the village which was all he could offer her now. That it was

166

unattractive and mediocre he very well knew, but as a doctor's house it served his purpose. It was conveniently situated, too. But neither of these recommendations could be expected to appeal to Diana.

She was gay tonight and soon he was sharing her mood, his doubts and dark speculations banished. There was an intimacy in her smile—or was it an invitation? Either way, the effect was potent and disturbing and suddenly he wished that the evening was not to be shared with others, for he wanted to make love to her. And how could he until the other guests, whoever they might be, had gone?

'Diana,' he said urgently, 'let's cut the evening short. Get rid of the others. Be alone together . . .'

She looked at him in surprise, but a surprise which was both pleased and gratified. She put down her glass and came to him, sliding her long hands slowly up his lapels and over his shoulders until her fingers linked behind his neck and, slowly, drew his head down to her own. And then she kissed him, lingering at the first soft touch of the lips and then pressing her mouth closer . . . closer . . . Her body, too: He could feel the pressure of her hips against his own; thigh against thigh. And suddenly the heady proximity overcame him and he swept her close, kissing her with deep and unrestrained desire.

'Diana . . . Diana!'

If you did but know, she thought complacently, you're doing the very thing I willed you to do; reacting the very way I planned!

A sudden elation ran through her. It was as easy as this to get what she wanted! As easy as this to influence him! So why should she be afraid of him meeting Sally again? He could never be attracted to anyone so ordinary. Sally was a milk-and-water creature, incapable of inspiring passion in a man—especially a man like this.

Confidence ran through Diana. She wasn't afraid of Sally! Why had she ever been? She was afraid of nothing and no one. She felt Christopher's lips against her hair and heard his voice whispering urgently: 'Get rid of them, Diana, whoever they are. Ring them up now—make some excuse and put them off!'

She laughed indulgently, but a little exultantly.

'Darling, how can I? It's too late. They'll be here any moment.'

'In that case I'll make the most of these precious minutes. And for heaven's sake break the evening up swiftly and spend the rest of it alone with me.'

He heard her breathless little laugh and caught her close again. They were oblivious of everything but each other. Therefore, the sound of a car engine took some little time to register.

Diana heard it first, and broke away abruptly.

'Here they are, Christopher! No, no—not again! Later . . .'

She moved swiftly across the room to tidy her hair before an ornate gilt mirror.

But when Sally stood upon the threshold of the open french windows she was not deceived. They stood apart—too far apart. They were casual—too casual. They've been making love, she thought, and wondered why she couldn't feel amused by their pretence.

Sally's unexpected appearance caught Christopher unawares, but his surprise and embarrassment were well concealed. She flashed him a friendly smile after greeting Diana, and said:

'Martin's just parking the car. He'll be with us in a minute. How elegant you look, Diana—forgive me for coming along in my workaday suit. I've come straight from the hospital.'

'Darling, you look very nice. As always.'

Sally caught sight of herself in a mirror. Very nice, she thought. That just about describes me. Unspectacular, ordinary, and dull.

Conversation flowed easily. There was no tension in the atmosphere. They were four young people embarking upon an evening together, and Diana was the perfect hostess. But right from the beginning the pairing-off was established and by the time they finally parted—not as early as Diana had planned

169

and Christopher had wanted—a further date had been fixed. The Hospital Ball, a fortnight hence. 'Why don't we repeat this foursome?' Martin had suggested, and so it was arranged there and then.

It wasn't until later that Diana wondered why Christopher had made no move to curtail the evening, or to remind her of his desire to be alone with her. And he hadn't driven to St. Mawes—he'd left her to do that, apparently quite content to chat over his shoulder to Martin and Sally as she did so. It didn't mean anything, of course, and it helped to launch the evening on an easy footing. Perhaps that was why he did it. From then on conversation had flown easily and smoothly. It was just as if there had never been any tension or embarrassment between them; no hurt or animosity. Christopher and Sally didn't seem the least self-conscious with each other—or particularly aware of each other. So Diana knew that the past was well and truly past and that she had nothing to fear from the future.

Christopher didn't avoid conversation with Sally, but he didn't seek it, either. Topics were bandied between the four of them, light-heartedly. Only once, when Diana lingered over her make-up in the cloakroom after dinner and Sally returned to the two men, did any personal discussion take place between them, and then but briefly.

It was Sally who launched it, quite

impulsively.

'Chris, I hope you didn't think I was visiting your patient yesterday in any way but a social one?'

Remembering his reaction to the sight of her car parked outside the Blundell cottage, he felt a fleeting shame.

'Of course not,' he hastened to assure her, and his face was suddenly lit by a warm and friendly smile. 'Actually, I was glad to see you there. Young Mrs. Blundell needs a reassuring friend just now. She's rather scared about this baby, you know.'

'Are there likely to be complications?'

'Only if a premature birth occurs. The position of the child isn't favourable for that.'

Sally felt suddenly at ease and aware of a deep sense of gladness because they were talking to each other. She forgot Martin, standing by, watching and listening. She forgot everything but a sudden desire to be friends with the man who had worked with her father, the man he had admired so much. She heard herself saying: 'Chris, I'm sorry for the way I behaved over your appointment. I was jealous, I suppose, just plain jealous. I said some beastly things, too. Will you forgive me?'

His smile was even warmer.

'My dear, I've nothing to forgive. Your reaction was natural and inevitable. *I'm* the one to ask forgiveness, but please believe that had I known you intended to apply for the

171

practice, I would never have done so.'

She felt her hand suddenly clasped in both of his, and was wildly, and ridiculously, happy.

'But what made you think I didn't intend to?' she asked curiously. 'Surely you knew all we had planned together, my father and I?'

'I thought you had abandoned those plans—'

'*Abandoned* them?'

'For marriage. I understood you were going to marry Martin and give up medicine.'

'So she is,' Martin cut in coldly. 'And the sooner the better.'

Sally checked a swift retort by biting her lower lip sharply. She wanted to ask Christopher why he had assumed so much, but said nothing. The evening had been an enjoyable one, crowned by this sudden renewal of their friendship, so why spoil it? The past was past. And, besides, what Martin said was probably true. Whom else would she marry, but him?

And then Diana was coming towards them, unaware of the sudden tension between Martin and Christopher.

'Shall we go on and dance somewhere?' she said gaily. 'There's that new place in Falmouth Bay—'

But Sally said: 'It sounds lovely, Diana, but I'm on duty early tomorrow morning. I must get to bed at a reasonable hour tonight.'

'Me, too,' said Christopher.

He seemed to have forgotten the beginning

of the evening and his desire to spend it alone with Diana. When they returned to The Towers, Christopher merely stayed for a nightcap with the others, then drove back with them to the village. A disappointing ending, thought Diana, but it didn't matter. She had had those moments in Christopher's arms, and very revealing moments had they been. He couldn't have forgotten them so soon.

She was pleased, too, because she had heard no reference to his acquisition of Dr. Peterson's practice and presumed that the subject had been forgotten. Sally had accepted the situation. She had recovered from her anger. And Martin seemed very sure of her. As sure as she herself was of Christopher.

CHAPTER THIRTEEN

To Diana's surprise, Sally telephoned her the next day asking for the address of her clever little dressmaker.

'I wondered if she could make something fairly quickly, something for the Hospital Ball?'

Sally wondered, as always, why she was weak enough to confide in Diana. Why didn't she just ask for the woman's address without revealing why she wanted it? To have something made for the ball lent too much importance to it. No wonder Diana's laughter tinkled down the line.

'Darling, do you think a local hop is worth it? Surely you've got something that would do—then you could spend the money on a new suit or something.'

To replace my neat little navy, thought Sally with an inward smile. Well, I suppose that would be more sensible.

But she had set her heart, suddenly and inexplicably, upon a new dance dress.

'I'm a member of the medical staff,' she retorted lightly. 'I can't let the hospital down by appearing in my old bronze lace.'

It sounded reasonable enough and Diana gave her the address without further comment.

But why did I feel that she didn't really want to? Sally wondered as she replaced the receiver.

But she forgot about Diana in the enjoyment of planning her new dress.

Charlotte Nicholls was certainly talented and had a fund of ideas—also, to Sally's surprise, a stock of enchanting materials. Failles, organzas, Swiss cottons, slipper satins, and brocades, all in exquisite colours and designs. With quick and eager hands the woman draped a selection over Sally's slim figure. She was enthusiastic and, had Sally but known it, pleased to have the order. She was anxious to build up a select clientele in a district which seemed to be divided into two classes, those with plenty of money and those with very little. A friend of Diana Langdon's would surely have plenty—and she was a doctor, too. That could mean further recommendations amongst the type of people she sought. So the shrewd Charlotte Nicholls secretly vowed that the gown would be one of the most exquisite she had ever made.

But she was dismayed by the girl's choice of colour. Young Dr. Peterson turned instinctively to the quiet ones—to soft blues and greys and pastel shades. Nothing that could possibly catch the eye. That, Charlotte decided, wouldn't do at all. She was out for business, so the gown had to be noticeable. Besides, in the right colours, Sally Peterson could be very striking. With unfailing intuition the woman produced a roll of slipper satin in a vivid peacock blue and draped it expertly across Sally's shoulders.

'There!' she said with satisfaction, and stood back, surveying the effect with pleasure.

'It's much too vivid!' Sally protested. 'I could never wear this!'

'Nonsense!' cried the determined Miss Nicholls, and turned Sally around to face a long mirror.

For a moment Sally stared in silence. The colour was spectacular and beautiful. It did something to her eyes and her hair and her skin. She felt a little breath of excitement, and smiled.

'What did I tell you?' said Charlotte Nicholls. 'This is the colour you should wear for evening. In fact, you should wear vivid colours always, because you're a vivid sort of person.'

Sally laughed uncertainly. 'Not I!' she protested.

'If you really believe that, then it's about time you wakened up to yourself, if I may say so. Look in that mirror again—'

But Sally hadn't stopped looking. She was enchanted and more than a little tempted, but in the secret corners of her heart she was also a little frightened, for it would take courage to appear in Tresanton wearing such a colour as this. But suddenly she knew that she was going to.

Martin wouldn't like it, of course, but she thrust that thought aside. Martin was too reserved. Perhaps she was a little too reserved herself. In childhood and girlhood she had worn the drab browns and navies and serviceable colours which Martha, a shrewd housekeeper, chose with an eye for wear and durability. As a medical student she'd had no money at all for clothes, and as a house-physician she had invested what little she had in good, quiet colours which were so useful in a doctor's life.

But this was different. This was special. This was to be the first real ball gown she had ever had. And suddenly she knew that in this

176

talented woman's hands it would be wonderful. A dream gown—something she would remember all her life and perhaps look back upon as a kind of turning point, marking the end of her old, quiet, subdued existence.

She knew it was ridiculous to feel this way— ridiculous to attach so much importance to a mere hospital dance. She'd attended plenty in London. Bigger balls—more spectacular. And it hadn't mattered in the least what she wore. She'd always enjoyed herself for she had been popular at St. Mark's. And yet, this local hospital ball in a little Cornish town had suddenly assumed importance in her mind— or was it in her heart?

Walking home from Tresanton station she faced the fact squarely. The dance was important to her because Christopher was to be there. That was the truth of it and she had to acknowledge it. It even frightened her a little. She wasn't attracted by Christopher, was she? How could she be, when she hardly knew the man? She'd given him little opportunity to even get upon a friendly footing, so of *course*, she wasn't attracted to him!

Her footsteps quickened, as if anxious to get away from her own disturbing thoughts. But one fact was inescapable. This dance had not mattered in the least until it had been arranged that the four of them should go together. But Christopher would be partnering Diana and she, as always, would be teamed up with Martin—and she didn't want to be. The realisation made her feel suddenly guilty. She had always been happy enough in Martin's company, so why should she feel now that it was only the ties of habit which bound her to him—habit, plus the fact that everyone in Tresanton, her father included, had taken their partnership for granted? And I don't *like* being taken for granted, Sally thought suddenly and rebelliously, even though she knew she was being unjust to Martin in thinking so. If she hadn't wanted to be teamed up with him she should have discouraged him long ago.

She knew suddenly that the time had come to take stock of herself—and of the future. It wasn't fair to Martin to keep him dangling for ever. It wasn't fair to postpone or evade issues which concerned another person's life as well as her own. But she had been fond enough of him until she came home for good—until she returned to meet her father's locum and to find him the most compelling, the most disturbing, and the most infuriating man she had ever met in her life.

She thought with a touch of panic: This is ridiculous! He's in love with Diana. I know he's in love with Diana and it's perfectly obvious that Diana is in love with him.

But even that thought didn't prevent her from being most disturbingly aware of him.

She had reached the main part of the

village, and the street in which he lived. She saw the tall row of Victorian houses, and his front door, which was painted white, showing up clearly in the dusk. At that precise moment it opened and a young man appeared. He stood for a moment in the aperture and she recognised the broad shoulders of Jim Blundell and, beyond him, the even taller and broader figure of Christopher.

She hoped she could get by without being seen. But this was not to be, for as Jim turned and descended the steps, Christopher saw her passing the gate.

He waved a hand in greeting and hurried to meet her.

'You wouldn't be about to pay a social call, would you?' he asked with a smile, and she had to admit that she was on her way home from Falmouth and had just come off the train.

'Then a drink would do you good,' he insisted. 'And after that I'll drive you home.' Without waiting for a reply, he led her up the steps and into his house.

'Wasn't that Jim Blundell?' she asked.

Christopher nodded. 'He's worried about his wife.'

'Aren't things going too well with her?'

'Well, unless anything unforeseen happens nothing *should* go wrong. But they're very much in love,' Christopher said gently, 'and his anxiety is understandable.'

Sally looked around her with appreciation.

She was in a book-lined room—the very sort of room she had expected to see. There were faded rugs and a couple of shabby armchairs.

Christopher indicated one with a smile. 'Second-hand,' he said, 'but comfortable. I can promise you that.'

Sally sank into the chair gratefully. It had been a busy day at the hospital and the long session with the dress-maker had done little to ease her fatigue, exciting as it had been. She kicked off her shoes with a little sigh of relief and let her head fall back against a cushion. She was completely unselfconscious and Christopher, as he poured the drinks, thought what a relief it was to be with a girl who could relax—who could kick off her shoes and rumple her hair without wondering what sort of an impression she was making.

He felt a swift sense of disloyalty, aware that he was mentally comparing her with Diana, who was always so beautiful and so perfect and who would never be caught out. Of course, it was ridiculous to compare the two girls. Diana was just naturally beautiful and Sally was, well, just Sally. And although she didn't mean anything to him, he was glad to have her here and realised that for a long time he had been wanting to invite her—to see her in this very room just as she was now, relaxed and friendly, with no antagonism.

He said impulsively: 'I'm glad I met you, Sally—glad you're here in my house.'

180

'Why?' she asked curiously, hoping that the sudden acceleration of her heart had not increased the colour in her cheeks.

He shrugged evasively. 'Perhaps because my friendship with your father makes me want to be friends with his daughter, too. We were once, when we first met. Remember?'

'We didn't have the chance to become real friends,' Sally pointed out. 'We saw very little of each other.'

'Then can't we make up for it now?'

'I'd like that,' she said honestly. 'I'd like it very much.' Suddenly she smiled. 'Martha would, too.'

He laughed and asked how Martha was.

'Why don't you come and see for yourself some time?' Sally suggested spontaneously. 'You know she'd always have a welcome for you.'

He smiled at that, remembering his last visit to Creek House. It had been Martha alone who had welcomed him then.

'I'll say "hallo" to her when I take you back, if I may?'

Sally was about to protest that there was no need to drive her the short journey around the creek, and then suddenly refrained. She wanted him to take her home. She wanted to see him inside Creek House again. And, this time, to make him welcome.

'If you're not doing anything, Christopher, you could stay to supper. Martha would be

181

delighted, I know.'

'And you?' he asked, quietly.

'I should like it, too.'

'Then I need no further persuasion!'

Before they left he showed her over his house. He had worked wonders with the place. Sally remembered it as the gaunt and chilly residence of one of her father's most irascible patients—a man who had never spent a penny on the place. But, within his limited means, Christopher had done more than that. He had painted and decorated, knocked up shelves, and transformed the back room into a well-equipped surgery.

She congratulated him and he said with a wry smile:

'After Creek House I must say this seems a bit bleak. But I've made the best of it, I think.'

'You certainly have.' She added impulsively: 'Why don't you invite Martha to see it some time? I believe she worries about you, you know. She's quite convinced that no bachelor could possibly make a home for himself.'

'I'll invite her on one condition. That you come, too.'

'All right,' she answered lightly, 'it's a promise. Invite us to tea sometime, and we'll both come.'

'In that case, I'll fix a date tonight.'

They were completely at ease with each other. She was no longer disturbed by him, and even wondered why she ever had been. He was just an amiable and friendly young man, not particularly good-looking and really no more attractive than Martin. Not in looks, at least.

Martha's smile, when she saw them together, was radiant.

'Doctor Maynard's come to share supper with us,' Sally told her blithely, avoiding the old lady's eye.

'And about time, too,' Martha declared, implying that the invitation, as far as Sally was concerned, was long over-due.

The woman bustled away happily to the kitchen. There'd be no supper on a tray for Miss Sally tonight, thank goodness. No solitary meal on a trolley. There was the dining-room table to lay and silver to put out. It would be just like old times, she thought contentedly, and was aware of a sudden hope in her maternal heart. This was as it should be— young Dr. Maynard and Sally Peterson beneath one roof together. If she had her way, and she frankly admitted that she wanted it, they'd share the same roof for always. And how Diana Langdon would dislike *that*! Martha thought with satisfaction. If she knew he was here right now she'd soon be ringing up, or dropping in. She never misses anything, that one! But this was something she was going to miss. This was Miss Sally's night—and about time, too!

But it wasn't a particularly exciting evening—just quiet and contented. Martha served a good and homely meal, as always, and the two young people enjoyed every mouthful. And afterwards they sat beside the fire, just talking—but finding a mighty lot to talk about, Martha observed to herself. Maybe things would progress from here to a little more action and less conversation!

It was the happiest evening that Sally had known since her father's death. Suddenly the past had come to life again. The house itself had come to life again, with the old feeling of companionship and happiness that had been missing until tonight. And when, later, Christopher rose reluctantly, Sally accompanied him to the front door and looked across the garden to the still waters of the creek.

'I'm glad you came, Christopher,' she said quietly.

'I'm glad, too. We're friends again, aren't we? Permanently this time, I hope.'

She looked up at him and smiled.

'I hope so, too.'

Suddenly he stooped and kissed her. Lightly, briefly, but disturbingly.

'That's to put a seal upon it,' he said softly, and a moment later he had gone.

She watched his car disappear down the drive and then turned and went inside. Quietly she closed the door and leaned against it. She was glad Martha had gone to bed. She wanted to be alone, for she was trembling—trembling

184

with a sudden terrifying awareness. If this was the effect so light a kiss could have upon her, then she could never marry Martin. It would be wrong to marry him, for his kisses never did this to her. She accepted them from habit and because they comforted her. And in a quiet, unexciting way, she enjoyed them.

'But I don't *love* him,' she thought suddenly, and passionately. 'I don't love him and I can't marry him and I've got to tell him so!'

But she couldn't tell him why—for that was something she wouldn't even acknowledge to herself.

CHAPTER FOURTEEN

Martin was startled when he saw the new dress. Sally swept downstairs and caught him unawares. He was standing in the drawing-room, facing the fire, and at the sound of her footstep he turned eagerly and then was silent.

Sally pirouetted gracefully. 'Well,' she cried gaily, 'do you like it?'

'Like it!' Martin stammered: 'It's—it's—' He laughed a little breathlessly. 'It's wonderful, but really, Sally, do you think you ought to wear a thing like that? Just now, I mean?'

She felt chilled. 'Just now?' she echoed. 'Why, just now?'

'Well—it isn't so long since your father died.'

A sudden anger beat with urgent wings against her heart. She lifted her head a little proudly and answered:

'I think my father would be happy if he knew I was wearing a dress like this. I wish he could see me in it. Martha says it's wonderful.'

'Oh, it is—it is!' he hastened to assure her. 'But not *you*, somehow.'

'But what is "me" Martin? Something subdued, and quiet, and ladylike, and negative?'

He saw that he had annoyed her and hastened to make amends.

'I didn't mean that, Sally, but, dash it all, you took me by surprise.' His eyes swept over her with reluctant admiration. 'It's a bit daring, isn't it? I've never seen you wear anything as low as that.'

She laughed, her anger suddenly gone.

'Would you say it was daring if Diana wore it?'

'Of course not. But—she's not like *you*.'

Suddenly, Sally wasn't amused any more.

'Don't be so stuffy, Martin!' she said impatiently.

He ruffled a little at that. 'Well, I won't be the only one in Tresanton who'll be surprised,' he said huffily. 'What's come over you, Sally?'

'Nothing's come over me,' she retorted lightly and, crossing to a cabinet, took out

186

bottles and glasses.

Martin watched her moodily. She hadn't greeted him very enthusiastically, he felt. Dash it all, he thought, I haven't even had a chance to kiss her! But when he tried to rectify that she side-stepped him.

'Here are the others!' she cried, as if glad of an excuse to evade him.

It had been arranged that Diana and Christopher should call for Sally and Martin at Creek House. And now Diana entered in a whirl of white tulle and sparkling sequins. She looked beautiful, as always, but for a brief moment she stood and stared at Sally.

'My word!' she said softly. 'You look pretty spectacular tonight. What's come over you?'

Sally laughed a little self-consciously. 'Your clever little dressmaker,' she said. 'You must give her all the credit.'

Christopher, who had been parking the car in the drive, joined them at that moment. He looked very striking in evening dress. Quite different from the tweed-clad doctor who drove around the country lanes in a shabby old car. In fact, he and Diana made a very striking couple.

Diana moved quickly into the drawing-room, but not quickly enough to miss Christopher's greeting for Sally. It wasn't so much what he said, but the way he looked. For a moment he said nothing at all, but stood regarding her in admiration.

'You look very beautiful, Sally. I like your gown.'

'Thank you, Christopher.'

'Your father would have liked it, too.'

She flashed him a grateful smile.

'You might tell Martin that.'

'Why? Doesn't he like it?'

'He doesn't quite approve. In fact, I'm not so sure that Tresanton itself is going to approve!'

'If it doesn't, Sally, you can put it down to sheer bad taste—or jealousy.'

She threw back her head and laughed. 'Ridiculous,' she said. 'No one would ever be jealous of me!'

'There has to be a first time for everything,' he said, and followed her to the drawing-room, where Martin greeted him affably and handed him a glass.

Until that moment Christopher had felt very much at home, very much at ease. He always had the feeling that he belonged there, which was ridiculous, of course, because he had only spent six months in this house and Martin had been coming and going all his life. Now he officiated as host, as if occupying his rightful and natural place.

Diana raised her glass and said: 'Here's to a successful evening. May we all enjoy ourselves. You certainly look as if you mean to, Sally.' She turned to the two men and finished: 'Isn't Sally looking spectacular tonight?'

'I think she looks very beautiful,' Christopher answered.

'So do I, darling. Very beautiful. Sally, you should wear that colour more often.'

'So Charlotte Nicholls said.'

'The woman has good taste, I will say that for her, but I hope she didn't rook you too much?'

Sally was so startled that she was glad when Christopher answered for her.

'Whatever you paid for that dress, Sally, it was worth it.'

'Thank you, Christopher. I'm afraid Martin doesn't care for it very much.'

'Oh, I didn't say that exactly,' Martin protested. 'I just think it isn't *you*, Sally. I was a bit startled when you came in.'

'Because you expected the old bronze lace,' said Sally, gently. 'Well, I don't blame you, Martin. All the same, I can't tell you how glad I am to be rid of it.'

'Your father always liked it,' he said a little gruffly.

'Father, bless him, thought I looked nice in anything. I still think he would have liked me in this. Christopher thinks so, too.'

'I do, indeed,' Christopher echoed.

Diana said a little briskly, 'Shall we go? I don't want to miss any of the dancing, even if it *is* only a village hop.'

For some inexplicable reason that remark annoyed Sally. She had always regarded these local affairs in the same category, yet now she sensed a patronage, even a contempt, in Diana's voice. She didn't like it. She checked an instant retort, but Christopher sensed her' reaction and understood it.

He said quietly: 'I wouldn't class the Hospital Ball as a village hop, Diana.'

She shrugged. 'Oh well, you know what I mean—compared with dances in London it *is* only a country affair . . .'

Which suggests that I have been silly and vain and extravagant, Sally reflected, squandering money on a lavish dress when a simple one would have been better.

Not that Diana's dress was particularly simple—but then everyone expected her to be spectacular, just as everyone expected she, Sally Peterson, to be homely, quiet and dull.

A sudden wave of determination leapt within her. I'm going to enjoy myself tonight, she vowed. No matter what Diana thinks or says, I'm going to have a *wonderful* time!

And so she did. It was an evening she would remember all her life, one in which she laughed and joked and danced with carefree abandon; one in which she found Christopher's arm about her waist not once, not twice, but many times. An evening through which Martin glowered and, when he danced with her, showed his disapproval in every stiff, unyielding inch.

Once she tried to coax him out of it. 'Come

190

on, Martin,' she leaded. 'Unbend.'

'I don't know what you mean,' he answered stiffly.

Her gay little laugh infuriated him. He had never seen Sally in this mood before. He had grown to rely upon her. She had always run true to the conventional pattern of which he and his family thoroughly approved. She was what his mother always called a 'ladylike' girl. That was the way he thought of her himself, and that was the way he wanted her. Not that she was being unladylike exactly, but she certainly wasn't being herself tonight—not the girl *he* knew, anyway.

And so he sulked his way through the evening, refusing to admit that his discontent was due to jealousy. She dance far too often with young Doctor Maynard, who was a nice enough fellow, of course, and one who had settled down very well in this tight, conservative little village, but Martin hadn't been aware of any particular friendship between him and Sally before. On the contrary, he'd always believed that she thoroughly disliked the man. Yet now she seemed to have recovered from her resentment of him—recovered to such a degree that they even appeared to be on intimate and friendly terms.

Diana observed this, too, and didn't like it. It was true that she had wanted to renew her friendship with Sally, but mainly to find out just how she and Christopher behaved together. Now that she saw it she wasn't very pleased. But Diana was careful to hide her feelings, a thing of which Martin was incapable, and since Diana never lacked partners it might appear to onlookers that Christopher was dancing with Sally only because he couldn't dance continuously with herself. Diana hoped that everyone would put this interpretation upon things, but it was obvious to her that Christopher and Sally thoroughly enjoyed being together.

'Why don't you cut in?' she said softly to Martin when, very briefly, she was sitting out. She had just finished an exhausting duty-dance with a local town-councillor and was glad to return to her table for a drink. Martin was sitting there morosely surveying the dance floor, twirling a glass in his hand. He looked like a spoilt and sulky small boy and a wave of irritation swept through her. If this was how he behaved, no wonder Sally was stalling over their marriage!

'If you don't look out,' she said quietly, 'you'll lose her altogether.'

He jerked to attention. 'Lose her? Sally, you mean? Don't be ridiculous.'

'It's *you* who is being ridiculous,' she answered tartly, 'wearing your heart upon your sleeve the way you do. Do you imagine everyone in this ballroom isn't aware that you're angry and jealous?'

'Jealous of what?' he scoffed.

'Of the fact that Sally's proving very popular tonight.'

For a moment his eyes met hers.

'I'm not the only one who's jealous.'

She coloured a little at that, then shrugged negligently.

'I've not the slightest cause to be jealous of Sally, and well you know it. But success seems to have gone to her head tonight. It must be the new dress. Secretly, Martin, I agree with you—it isn't the sort of dress Sally should wear.'

'But Christopher Maynard admired it,' he said pointedly.

'He was being polite, that's all.'

Martin laughed, shortly.

'You know that isn't true; Diana.'

'Then why don't you *do* something about it?' she retorted angrily. 'Cut in. Take her away from him. After all, you *are* going to marry her, aren't you?'

'Of course. Everyone knows that.'

'Well, judging from the way she's behaving tonight it doesn't seem to be particularly apparent to *her.*' Diana leaned across the table suddenly and laid her hand upon his sleeve. There was an urgency in her touch—and a sympathy, too, for which he was grateful. 'Martin, why don't you assert yourself? You know Sally's only killing time in this house-physician's job. Where will it get her?'

'Nowhere,' he answered abruptly. 'Don't

think I haven't pointed that out to her dozens of times.'

'Talking never got a man anywhere, Martin. It's actions that count. The trouble with you is that you're too much of a gentleman.'

To her surprise Martin retorted: 'What you mean is that I'm too settled—settled in a nice comfortable rut. Maybe you're right. It's about time I did jerk out of it, and Sally with me.'

Diana's hand gave his own an encouraging squeeze. 'Now you're talking, Martin. Go on, cut in right now! Take her away from Christopher.'

'My dear Diana, that sort of thing isn't done!'

She laughed at him. 'Not here in Tresanton, perhaps, but it's a transatlantic custom which is rapidly creeping in. And it has its uses. Go ahead and try it.'

Reluctantly, and with a touch of bravado, he got to his feet, stalked across the dance floor and tapped Christopher on the shoulder.

'Do you mind if I cut in?' he queried amiably.

'I mind very much,' Christopher answered, and whirled Sally away.

Martin had never felt such a fool in his life. He turned on his heel, stalked back to the table and faced Diana, his mouth a tight line of anger.

'Satisfied?' he snapped.

'It was your own fault. You weren't firm

194

enough.'

They sat together in frozen silence until the dance ended and Sally and Christopher rejoined them. Christopher's hand was beneath Sally's elbow—quite unnecessarily, Diana thought.

She rose abruptly as the couple reached the table. 'I'm tired, I want to go home,' she said abruptly. 'Let's get our coats before the crush, Sally.' And without giving her time to answer Diana swept away.

There was nothing Sally could do but follow. She didn't want to terminate the evening. She'd had a wonderful time, but she smiled at the two men and said: 'We'll be with you in a minute,' and followed Diana towards the ladies' cloakroom.

There was no one there but an old village woman dozing amongst the hats and coats. Diana was powdering her nose and re-touching her lipstick as Sally entered.

'Enjoyed yourself, darling?' she asked sweetly.

'Very much,' Sally answered enthusiastically. 'I've had a wonderful time.'

'I'm so glad.' She sounded as if she meant it, too. 'You seem very popular with the hospital staff.'

'I hope so,' Sally answered.

Conversation lagged between them. Sally burrowed amongst the piled coats and salvaged her own, not wanting to disturb the old woman. The coat, compared with her dress, was uninteresting, but that didn't matter. She slung it carelessly over her shoulders so that a flame of peacock blue showed in startling comparison.

Diana yawned.

'Personally, I always find these local affairs rather dreary. The same old faces, the same old dresses—not that one could say that about *you* tonight.'

There was nothing Sally could say to that, so she didn't bother to answer.

Diana slipped into her mink coat and wrapped it around her luxuriously. 'Oh, for a good night's sleep!' she said. 'I'm tired. It's boredom, I think. Never mind, I've got the weekend to look forward to.'

'Are you doing something special then?' Sally asked with polite interest.

Diana's mouth curved into a smile—a smile of anticipation, it seemed to Sally. A significant sort of smile.

'Something *very* special,' Diana confided. 'I'm going home with Christopher for the weekend.'

'Home?' Sally echoed, puzzled.

'To Yorkshire, to meet his aunt. The aunt who brought him up. Maybe you've never heard of her.'

'Of course, I have. His Aunt Helen. She put him through medical school, Father told me.'

'That's true. Quite a rich old girl I think, in

her way. And Christopher's very devoted to her. She's been a mother to him all his life. That's why he wants me to meet her.'

'How nice,' said Sally inadequately, wondering if there were any particular reason for this visit and knowing, suddenly, that there was.

Diana said softly, 'All I hope is that the old girl approves of me.'

'Approves of you, Diana? Why?'

'Because it's important to Christopher that his aunt should like his wife.'

There was a stunned moment of silence, then Sally heard her voice echoing with a jerk: 'His—wife?'

'Oh, not yet, darling! We haven't run off and been married secretly, if that's what you're thinking. When it happens there'll be nothing secret about it! Father will see to that. He'll demand a big, slap-up wedding with all the trimmings—and I shan't mind just so long as I marry Christopher.'

'I didn't know you were engaged,' Sally said with an effort.

'It hasn't been announced yet, darling. You're the first person I've confided in. But it will be announced after I've met Christopher's aunt. Dear Christopher,' she continued tenderly, 'I believe he's quite a conventional man at heart and wants to do things in the right way.'

So it was as serious as that, Sally thought

197

bleakly. And that was why Christopher had been unable to invite Martha and herself to tea this weekend—the question of the proposed visit had come up, as he resolved, the night he had dined at Creek House. 'Sally says you don't believe any bachelor can make a home for himself,' he'd laughingly chided the old woman, 'so she insists that you come and see my house.'

Martha's broad face had beamed with delight.

'Why, Doctor, I'd like that very much.'

'Will you come to tea with Sally,' he'd asked, 'and make it soon?'

'I will that! Next weekend, if you like.'

But at that he had withdrawn. 'Not next weekend,' he said. 'I'm sorry, but I'm keeping that free.'

He didn't say why and Sally had foolishly presumed that work was the reason.

How wrong I was! she thought unhappily. How terribly wrong! He was taking Diana to Yorkshire to meet his aunt—to introduce to her the girl he was going to marry.

CHAPTER FIFTEEN

Sally said with an effort and, to her surprise, without a tremor in her voice: 'Congratulations, Diana.'

And Diana retorted sweetly: 'It's the man you congratulate, darling.'

Sally laughed. 'Of course. Well, lots of happiness, then.'

'Thank you, Sally.'

Diana was suddenly radiant again, and throughout the drive home she chattered animatedly, sitting beside Christopher in the front with Martin and Sally behind. Martin's arm was linked possessively through Sally's and she felt too stunned and sick to withdraw. All the delight of the evening had gone and behind her eyes she felt the prick of unshed tears.

So it was true, after all. Diana and Christopher were in love, they were going to be married, and she had been a fool to misinterpret Christopher's attention tonight. It was no more than that of a friend, of a man who had admired and respected her father. Only in her imagination had there been something more beneath his smile.

When they reached Creek House, Sally issued a conventional invitation to come in for a good night drink, but Diana, still pleading tiredness, declined. And that, of course, went for both, herself and Christopher.

Martin was glad, for he wanted to be alone with Sally. He was now in a determined mood and wasn't going to waste an opportunity.

Christopher held out his hand. 'Good night, Sally.'

She put her own into it and felt the warmth and strength of his touch. Her hand trembled for a moment and, afraid that he would notice, she pulled her fingers away and answered lightly: 'Good night. It's been a lovely evening.'

For a moment he regarded her thoughtfully. The moonlight etched her face with the cool precision of a cameo. She looked pale, he thought, paler than she had looked all night. Her face had been lit with an animation and vivacity which had attracted him, but now it was chilled and withdrawn; smiling at him courteously, but without warmth.

He said gently: 'I hope you're not on duty at the hospital tomorrow.'

'Why?' she jerked.

'Because it would do you good to have a rest.'

'Nonsense,' she retorted. 'I'm not in the least bit tired. It's Diana who's tired. You'd better take her home.'

And that was the end of the evening. She turned and ran lightly up the steps and unlocked the front door. A moment later she disappeared inside, with Martin at her heels.

Christopher drove away thoughtfully. After a while Diana looked at him and said: 'I'm still here, you know.'

He laughed. 'Did I seem so far away, Diana? I'm sorry.'

'You *were* far away,' she chided. But he made no attempt to explain his detachment, nor take her into his confidence.

* * *

Once alone with Sally, Martin said: 'I want to talk to you.'

'Not now!' she protested. 'It's late.'

'Not as late as it would have been had we stayed to the end of the dance. We left early, so that gives us a margin of time. And I think it's owing to me,' he added truculently.

'What do you mean, Martin?'

'Simply that I haven't seen much of you all evening.'

'Nonsense. We've danced together.'

'You know what I mean. We haven't been alone, and now that we are, I want to settle something.'

She felt a little arrow-thrust of alarm. She was not in the mood for a scene. She felt too stunned by Diana's news—news which had confirmed something she had known, in her heart, and refused to acknowledge. And now she must face it, and endure it.

Martin took hold of her shoulders and pulled her towards him. She stiffened at his touch and he said: 'What's the matter, Sally?'

'Nothing. Nothing at all.'

'That's not true. I know you well enough to be aware when you're unhappy, or when something is wrong.'

'Was this what you wanted to talk about?'

she asked with an effort.

'No—not precisely.'

'Then say what you have to say, Martin, and go—please.'

She was close to tears, to Martin's surprise. It wasn't like Sally to cry.

'Good heavens,' he said, 'I thought you'd been enjoying yourself!'

'I did enjoy myself.'

'Well, it doesn't look like it.' He put his arms about her again. 'Darling, what's the matter?'

She thrust him aside. 'Martin, *please*—'

At that his temper rose. 'Look here, Sally, I'm a patient man—'

That was true enough, she thought with an inner smile. He was too patient, perhaps. Her heart softened and she said: 'I'm sorry, Martin, but please go home.'

'Not until I've said what I want to say.' He looked truculent and resentful, like a small boy deprived of his own way.

Sally sank down wearily into an arm-chair. She didn't offer him a drink. She wasn't going to do anything to prolong the visit. She let her head fall back against the cushions, and closed her eyes.

'All right, Martin,' she said tiredly. 'Go ahead. I'm listening.'

'Not in a very receptive mood,' he retorted, 'but it doesn't matter. What I want settled between us, Sally, is the question of our

202

marriage.'

Briefly, she was silent and then, without opening her eyes, she said quietly: 'Is there any question about it?'

'Not as far as *I* am concerned, but I'm beginning to wonder as far as you are.'

She opened her eyes and looked at him. He saw compassion, and shame, and sadness mixed inextricably with tenderness. And the tenderness was for him, he knew that, although it worried him.

'I'm sorry, Martin,' she said quietly, 'I can't marry you.'

His face went rigid, not so much with shock as with anger.

'What the devil do you mean?' he demanded.

'Just that, Martin. I'm sorry, I can't marry you.'

'Why not?' he burst out. '*Why not?*'

'Because I don't love you.' When he didn't answer she continued swiftly: 'Forgive me, Martin, I should have told you before. I realised a few days ago. I think I should have realised long before that. But the fact is, I do know *now*. I don't love you—not enough for marriage.'

He looked so bereft that she cried: 'Forgive me, please. I didn't want to hurt you!'

But he wasn't so much hurt, as astonished.

'Do you expect me to believe this?' he demanded. And at that, all her fear and embarrassment and shame evaporated.

'You've got to believe it, Martin. I like you, I'm fond of you, but I don't *love* you.'

He asked abruptly: 'Why? Is there someone else—another man, I mean?'

She felt her heart pound with a sudden acceleration of alarm. At all costs he mustn't guess the truth—no one must know that. It was a thing she must lock in the deep recesses of her heart—a thing to bury, if she could, for ever.

'You know there isn't another man, Martin.'

'I know nothing of the sort—not after tonight!'

'Tonight has nothing whatever to do with it.'

'No?' he echoed. 'I'm not so sure about that.'

She ran a hand through her hair wearily. 'You can be sure about it, Martin, believe me. All this happened before tonight.'

'All *what* happened?' he echoed sharply.

She waved her hand helplessly, unable to explain.

'I mean the realisation that I didn't love you. I won't keep on repeating that I'm fond of you, because although it's true, I know it isn't enough.'

Martin said gruffly: 'It might be enough for me.'

'No, Martin. Not after we were married.'

'Perhaps you're attaching too much

importance to passion,' he said with a touch of embarrassment. 'But as to that, you needn't worry, Sally. I'm not a demonstrative man, if you know what I mean.'

'I'm afraid I do,' she answered with a little smile. 'And I do attach importance to passion. Don't look so embarrassed,' she added a little sharply. 'The physical side of love isn't something to whisper about, or blush over. It's a real and vital part of it—it's the demonstration of love. So unless I felt deeply and strongly attracted to a man I could never respond to him physically.'

He assumed an air of tolerant understanding, which jarred upon her.

'Look here, my dear, I'm older than you, and more experienced. I think you're attaching too much importance to the wrong things. I'm quite sure that, after we're married, everything will be all right—if you know what I mean.'

'I don't think I do,' she answered shortly. 'I've tried to be frank with you. Why don't you be the same with me?'

'It's all so embarrassing,' he protested. 'One doesn't discuss things like sex—'

'Why not, Martin? I'm a doctor, after all.'

'Oh, well, of course, if you're going to approach the whole thing clinically—'

Sally's laughter pealed. The sound of it startled and annoyed him.

'I don't see what's so funny about it, Sally.'

'No, Martin, I'm afraid you don't. And

205

you're probably right. It isn't funny at all, so let's drop the discussion, shall we?'

But Martin proved unexpectedly stubborn. 'No,' he insisted. 'I want the whole thing settled right here and now.'

'It is settled as far as I am concerned.'

'But not as far as I am. You haven't answered my question.'

'What question, Martin?'

'*Is* there another man?'

'No,' she repeated.

'What about Christopher Maynard?'

'What about him, Martin?'

'Well, you seemed to be enjoying yourself with him tonight.'

'And what does that imply?'

'That you've forgotten your earlier animosity towards him to a surprising degree.'

'Perhaps that's a good thing.' She refused to be cornered, or pinned down. Suddenly he regarded her with almost wary suspicion.

'You've changed, Sally. You're different, somehow.'

'Nonsense, Martin. I'm still the same old Sally Peterson, whom Tresanton has known all her life, and taken for granted.'

'I haven't taken you for granted, Sally.'

'Oh, yes, you have. So has everyone. It's been assumed, ever since we were children, that when we grew up we would marry. We were childhood sweethearts, according to everyone in this village.'

206

'Including your father,' he retorted.

'Oh yes,' she admitted, 'Father, too. But were he here now, he would understand, I'm sure.'

He'd understand that you're being suddenly and unexpectedly difficult.'

'Difficult, Martin?'

'Very difficult and unreasonable. What ails you, Sally?'

'Oh, please, Martin, don't start again! Can't you just accept the truth? If you're angry with me, I'm sorry, but the fact remains that I can't marry you because I don't love you.'

He looked at her for a long moment, realising that it was useless to pursue the subject—for the present, at any rate.

He observed resentfully: 'I'm still convinced that there's something behind all this. And I'm not so sure that it isn't Doctor Maynard. Not that *that* will do you much good,' he added unkindly. 'Diana's hooked him well and truly.'

But she was determined not to discuss Christopher and Diana. She didn't want to be reminded of them. Also, she was afraid of giving herself away and that was something she was resolved not to do, for not even to herself would she admit that she was in love with Christopher.

She rose and went to the door and opened it. 'You left your coat in the hall,' she said, tiredly.

Martin followed, suddenly contrite. He

came up behind her, put his hand upon her bare shoulders and turned her round to face him. His touch meant nothing to her. But the touch of another man's arm around her waist had elevated her to a plane of happiness which she had never scaled before. Even his kiss of friendship, light and impersonal though it was, had stirred her as Martin's kisses had never done. These were only two things which emphasised the truth to her and they were the two things she had to forget. She meant nothing to Christopher. He wanted to be friends with her for her father's sake, that was all.

'Sally—' Martin began urgently, pleadingly.

But she withdrew. 'Good night, Martin, and forgive me.'

'That,' he said stubbornly, 'is something I cannot do. You've taken leave of your senses. Let's hope it's only temporary.'

The front door closed heavily behind him and Sally turned and went upstairs. For a long moment she stood at the window of her room, looking out across the quiet waters of the creek. The village lay in darkness. Occasionally down the main road came the flash of headlights as people went home from the hospital dance. And somewhere, amid the shadows, stood a tall Victorian terraced house—Christopher's house. Was he home yet, or was he lingering over a tender good night with Diana—making love to her,

208

anticipating the day when his love would be more fully demonstrated, when she would belong to him and be his wife?

Abruptly Sally drew the curtains, undressed blindly and got into bed. Martha was astonished, when she came in with morning tea, to see Sally's new dress abandoned carelessly upon the floor, a shimmering pool of peacock blue from which the girl had stepped unheedingly the night before.

'Why, Miss Sally,' she said, 'what on earth's come over you? Fancy treating a beautiful dress this way! Did you have a good time last night?' She looked at the girl's tousled head and added with a laugh: 'No need for me to ask *that*, judging by the way you clambered into bed, tossing your clothes aside in this careless fashion!'

She flung the curtains back with a flourish, letting in the strong morning light. Then, turning to the bed, she stood still abruptly, shocked at the pallor of Sally's face.

'Why, Miss Sally,' she said in concern, 'aren't you well? Did you eat something last night that upset you? Now why didn't you call me when you came home?' she demanded severely.

Sally accepted the cup of tea and answered sleepily: 'I'm perfectly all right, Martha.'

'Well, you don't look it. You look as if you haven't slept a wink.'

That was true, though Sally wouldn't admit

209

it. She had lain despairingly awake, listening to the old grandfather clock downstairs chiming away the hours, and thinking: Why can't I cure myself?

Or was there no cure for love?

CHAPTER SIXTEEN

For the next few days Sally worked unceasingly at the hospital, putting in extra hours of duty and willingly deputising for any member of the medical staff who wanted to knock off early. Work was her salvation and she was grateful for it. She tried not to think of Christopher. Fortunately a constant stream of out-patients demanded her attention, but most of them were patients of his sent along for treatment or X-ray. Some brought letters written in his strong, firm hand and the sight of it stirred her now as it had never done before.

She felt a crippling sense of despair. 'Physician heal thyself,' she quoted inwardly and ironically. But there was no cure for this. She was deeply and irrevocably in love with him and would always be. And in comparison with her feelings for him, her fondness for Martin paled to insignificance.

She knew she had done the right thing in breaking with Martin, in telling him the truth—or as much of it as was wise. For even if

Diana did marry Christopher, and obviously she was going to, Sally knew that she couldn't live with any other man. And it wasn't fair to Martin, no matter what persuasions he used; no matter how forcibly he refused to believe that she didn't love him; no matter how much he declared that fondness and companionship could be a good basis for marriage, she knew that that was not what she wanted. All or nothing, she thought helplessly. And it's all work for me from now on.

Driving home from the hospital one evening she saw a light in Stella Blundell's cottage and impulsively stopped. The girl was hanging curtains at the window of a little room above the front door—a room she was preparing for the coming child.

'You shouldn't be doing that,' Sally scolded, when Stella opened the front door. 'I saw your figure silhouetted against the window.'

Stella smiled and asked her in.

'Come and see the nursery,' she said eagerly, 'it's looking lovely.'

And it was. Stella and her husband had decorated it themselves and the curtains, a gay nursery chintz, were the finishing touch.

'But you be careful,' Sally scolded, eyeing the flimsy little step-ladder. 'Surely you could wait for your husband to come home to put these up for you?'

'But I wanted it to be a surprise for him!'

Sally lingered briefly and then went on her

211

way, aware, as she was so often aware after visiting Stella, of an envy in her heart—an envy which was now doubly strong. What sort of a nursery would Diana prepare for Christopher's children? she thought suddenly. Nothing so simple and homely as Stella's, of course. Something elaborate and expensive and perfect, but not created with the pride and devotion that Stella and Jim had put into theirs. Diana wouldn't make curtains of gay nursery chintz. Hers would be put into the hands of some expensive interior decorator. There would be a day nursery, and a night nursery, and an immaculate nurse to look after the children, who would be visited by their mother at certain hours, as if they were toys to be taken out and played with and then discarded.

'I'm jealous!' Sally chided herself fiercely. 'Just plain jealous.'

But she couldn't stop thinking about Diana. Today was Friday—was she travelling north with Christopher tonight? It was a long journey to undertake by road even in Diana's powerful car—they'd spend most of the weekend getting there and back! In fact, Sally thought suddenly, it's a long trip to make just for a weekend ...

But not, of course, for so important a weekend. Would the engagement be announced immediately on their return? she wondered. Why not? If Joseph Langdon approved and Christopher's aunt approved, there would be no reason to wait.

* * *

On Saturday Sally finished early at the hospital. She was off duty in the afternoon and drove home full of plans for the day ahead. She would take Martha to the market in Truro, and whilst there, get more bulbs for the garden. Hyacinths and spring flowers. The rockery needed replenishing, too. There was always plenty to do in a garden and, like her work at the hospital, it would keep her occupied.

The market in Truro was busy, as always, and Martha and Sally returned with the car laden with purchases. It was dusk by the time they reached Tresanton and as they entered the High Street, the figure of a young man loomed out of the shadows, running blindly in front of the car. Sally braked abruptly and wound down the window to protest. The next moment she was silent, recognising Jim Blundell. He looked agitated and frightened.

'What's the matter, Jim?' Sally called sharply.

He stumbled and pulled up abruptly. 'It's Stella! She fell off the step-ladder—hanging a picture on the nursery wall, without my knowing!' His voice shook. 'I'm just going to fetch Doctor Maynard.'

213

Sally opened the car door abruptly. 'Jump in,' she commanded. And when he obeyed she reversed the car and drove back the way she had come.

'Doctor Maynard's away for the weekend,' she explained. 'I'll take a look at Stella.'

She didn't pause to wonder whether it was the ethical thing to do. Someone had to go to Stella and the village doctor was away. She could take a look at the girl and then telephone the hospital, if necessary. Ethics and professional conduct aside, it seemed the right thing to do because it was the human thing to do.

But once inside the cottage Sally knew there was no time to spare for telephoning the hospital. She took one glance at the girl's writhing figure and said to Jim abruptly: 'Fetch Martha.'

Jim obeyed hurriedly. He was frightened, badly frightened. He was clumsy and helpless and panic-stricken. Sally was thankful when Martha's bulky figure filled the doorway.

'Hot water, Martha, and plenty of it. Quickly.'

Martha took in the situation at a glance. The baby was on the way. It was a premature birth and a risky one, Sally knew, in view of the complications for which Stella had come to the hospital to be X-rayed. But the girl couldn't be moved. Sally had to deliver the child herself— and pray that nothing would go wrong.

CHAPTER SEVENTEEN

Christopher never really knew why he returned to Tresanton by the road which took him past the Langdon Chalk Pits and the row of workers' cottages in which the Blundells lived. He was tired. He'd had a long day and now he was thinking of his fireside, his slippers, a tray with something appetising upon it, and a glass containing something stimulating. That was what he needed after his session with the Medical Board, a session which had begun early on Saturday morning and continued well into the afternoon. Then he had gone back to the local Medical Officer's house for a belated meal. After that there'd been one or two calls to make on his way home.

So when he reached the Blundells' cottage it was already dark. He saw with surprise, and quickening of pleasure, that Sally's car stood outside. But this time he didn't suspect the worst. He knew that Sally visited Stella on a friendly footing and that she was interested in the girl. So there was no reason to wonder why she was visiting his patient.

Perhaps it was the sight of Sally's car which persuaded him to call. As far as he knew, everything was proceeding quite satisfactorily with young Mrs. Blundell, but a call, even at this late hour, might reassure her worried young husband.

But the sight of Jim's face pulled Christopher up abruptly. The man was as white as a sheet, obviously frightened and worried.

'What's wrong?' Christopher said quickly, and Jim pointed mutely upstairs.

'She had a fall,' he stammered. 'A bad one. Doctor Peterson's with her now.'

Christopher raced upstairs. On the threshold of the bedroom he paused abruptly and Sally looked up, startled by the sound. Beads of sweat stood upon her forehead, but she was calm—utterly calm. Beside her stood Martha, obviously frightened, and in a detached corner of his mind Christopher was surprised that the capable Martha should panic in a moment of crisis. And this obviously was a crisis.

Christopher took in the situation at a glance and said briefly: 'I'll be with you in a minute,' and went to the bathroom to scrub up. When he returned the situation was unchanged. The birth was under way, but not normally.

'Martha, why don't you go downstairs and make that young man a strong cup of tea? And drink one yourself.'

She threw him a grateful glance before leaving the room. He smiled briefly at Sally and took his place beside her. She was thankful to see him. This was a case outside

216

her own experience and although the mother was being very plucky, she was nevertheless frightened. And a frightened patient was a handicap to any doctor.

Christopher stooped over Stella and said gently: 'Relax, my dear. There's nothing to worry about. Doctor Peterson's doing a marvellous job. Just you put your trust in us and everything will be all right.'

That was a long night. A night of tension and anxiety. A night in which Christopher and Sally worked together in one united effort. There was no time for conversation, no time for questions or explanations—no time for anything but the job in hand. And in the urgency of the moment it didn't even occur to Christopher to wonder how Sally came to be attending his patient. That thought only came to him later—much later.

Shortly after Christopher's arrival the birth reached a stage where it was safe to give the mother an anaesthetic and, after that, the only sound in the room was an occasional word of command from Christopher. And so the moments ticked by, tense and concentrated and anxious.

Christopher was aware that he had never worked with anyone as he did with Sally. They were united in thought and purpose. He was impressed by her gentleness and her deep concern for the mother and child and, she in turn, was impressed by his skill. He was a

217

wonderful doctor and she was deeply grateful for the chance to work with him. No wonder her father had praised him so highly—and no wonder, she thought, that he was appointed to the practice instead of me. He deserved to be.

During the night Jim Blundell took Martha home. Briefly, Sally was able to leave Christopher's side, and go downstairs. Martha was half asleep beside the kitchen fire, her head lolling forward wearily. Sally's heart was filled with compassion—also for Stella's husband, who was nervously smoking cigarette after cigarette.

'Stella's being very plucky,' she said, 'and she couldn't be in better hands than Doctor Maynard's, so try not to worry. Would you take Martha home? I'd like her to go to bed. My car is outside.'

The young man jumped up with alacrity, glad of something to do.

'You don't mind the walk back from Creek House, do you?' Sally asked. 'If you leave the car there I can drive back with Doctor Maynard.' She smiled and finished: 'Besides, the walk will do you good.'

Later—much later, it seemed to her—she heard the young man's returning footsteps; heard him moving about in the kitchen. And then there was silence. Had he fallen asleep by the kitchen fire? She hoped so.

The sky was streaked with dawn before—everything was over. Over safely and successfully, thanks to Christopher. Sally breathed a prayer of thankfulness that he had come in time. She couldn't have handled the case herself—not so skilfully and surely. As she took the tiny, premature scrap of humanity from Christopher's strong hands she said simply: 'You were wonderful—absolutely wonderful.'

He looked at her in surprise and said with a smile: 'Don't give *me* all the credit. You were pretty wonderful yourself, my dear. Thank you for your help.'

While Sally attended to the child, Christopher went downstairs to give the news to Jim. 'Everything's all right,' he said. 'Congratulations. You have a fine son.'

The young man was unable to speak. His eyes filled with tears as he inquired incoherently about his wife.

'She's asleep, and she'll be all right,' Christopher reassured him. 'All the same, I think it would be a good idea if we got her and the baby to hospital tomorrow. Just for a few days, for proper nursing. The birth was premature and the child will need a little extra attention. Your wife's come through a bad time, so for your own peace of mind I'll have them both moved to hospital first thing in the morning.'

There wasn't a telephone at the Blundells' cottage so Christopher telephoned the hospital from Sally's house. Whilst he did so she made coffee. He joined her in the kitchen, strolling in just as he had been accustomed to during his six months in this house.

'Everything's taken care of,' he said. 'An ambulance will collect her at nine o'clock and I've arranged for the district nurse to be there at six to do whatever is necessary.'

It wasn't until they were seated opposite each other, one on either side of the kitchen table, that Christopher said suddenly: 'What were you doing there, Sally? How did you come to be attending my patient?'

'Are you angry?' she asked.

'I ought to be, I suppose. It's completely unethical, you know.'

'Unethical? To attend an emergency?'

'I should have been fetched,' he pointed out reasonably.

'But you were away.'

'Only in Falmouth. My housekeeper could have got a message to me.'

He wanted to be angry, he would have been justified in being angry, but for one thing he was too tired, and, for another, he was too grateful. Sally had worked valiantly tonight.

He became aware that she had paused with her cup halfway to her mouth, and was staring at him with a sort of puzzled surprise.

'In Falmouth?' she echoed. 'But you were going to Yorkshire this weekend.'

It was his turn to stare. 'Yorkshire?' he echoed. 'Why on earth should I go to

220

Yorkshire—and for a weekend, too? Good heavens, it takes almost that time to get there!'

'But you were taking Diana—'

'Taking Diana?' he echoed. 'Now why should I take Diana to Yorkshire?'

'To meet your aunt.'

'Aunt Helen? But she hasn't even heard of her. I don't think I've ever mentioned Diana in my letters.'

'I—I must have misunderstood,' Sally said warily and tried to change the subject by offering him more coffee. But Christopher would not be side-tracked.

'What made you think I'd gone to Yorkshire with Diana?' he persisted. 'You couldn't have imagined a thing like that.'

'No,' she answered carefully, 'I didn't imagine it.'

'Then you were told it.'

'Yes.'

'By whom?'

What could she answer, but the truth?

'By Diana.'

'When?'

'At the dance the other night—in the cloakroom.'

'But what the devil made her tell you a thing like that?'

'I suppose—because she believed it. You must have given her good reason.'

For a moment Christopher didn't answer. He was baffled—and angry too. Angry, because this statement of Diana's was compromising and untrue.

'Sally,' he said abruptly, 'I want to tell you something, and I want you to believe it. I have never at any time asked Diana to meet my aunt.'

'You don't have to explain to me—' Sally, began quickly.

'I know I don't have to, but I want to. I know you wouldn't have attended a patient of mine unless you had good reason to believe that I was unavailable.'

'But you yourself said you weren't free this weekend.'

'When did I say that?'

'When we were arranging a date to bring Martha to tea, remember? You said you wouldn't be free this weekend. And then Diana told me you were taking her to Yorkshire, it all fitted in.'

'I wasn't free because the local Medical Officer wanted me to give evidence at a meeting of the Medical Board. He's been battling against Tresanton's sewage system and asked for my support, which I gave very readily. I kept this morning free for that and the meeting, which was specially called, went on longer than was expected.'

'Did you win?' she asked with a sudden smile.

'We won all right. But not without a battle. After that I went back to his house for a meal, made one or two calls, and was on my way home when I saw your car outside the Blundells' cottage. That was why I dropped in. While we are telling each other the truth, Sally, you may as well have it from me. I'd no idea Stella was ill when I called tonight. I wouldn't have done so if you hadn't been there. I wanted to see you.'

'Why?' she asked, breathlessly.

'I don't know. I just had a sudden desire to. Do you mind?'

'No. I'm glad.' She laughed and finished: 'Just how glad I was when I saw you standing at the bedroom door you'll never know!'

'And *you* will never know just what tonight meant to me. I've wanted to know you, really know you, for a long time, Sally, but I don't think anything could have brought us so close together as tonight has done.'

When Sally smiled her serious young face was transformed. He thought she had never looked so lovely as she did right now, with her hair dishevelled and her eyes shadowed through lack of sleep.

He said with sudden compunction: 'Go to bed, my dear. It's selfish of me to keep you up.'

At the door, he asked: 'Are you doing anything tomorrow?'

'Yes,' she answered, 'I've a couple of hundred bulbs to plant.'

'May I come and help you? I'd resolved to set tomorrow aside for some long overdue desk-work but I'd rather plant bulbs,' he said. 'Especially in this garden. I've a great affection for it, you know.'

'Then come any time you like,' she told him.

He was about to say: 'I'll come first thing in the morning,' then checked himself. There was something else he had to do. Something important. And that was to see Diana and to find out just why she had told Sally he was taking her to Yorkshire to meet his aunt.

CHAPTER EIGHTEEN

It was Joseph Langdon's custom to occupy a front pew in the village church every Sunday morning. This habit had helped to establish him as a respectable member of the community—a man to be trusted and accepted—and had gone a long way in furthering his ambition to become recognised as a leading social figure, as well as an industrial tycoon. In his youth he had not been a church-going man, but in middle-age the habit had acquired a dignity and an indefinable comfort.

He liked it even better when his daughter accompanied him, for he was proud of Diana, not only of her beauty but of her poise and assurance, the very qualities on which he had expended so much thought and hard-earned money.

But on the day following the birth of Stella Blundell's child, Diana complained fretfully that she had a headache. In a mood of paternal anxiety he urged her to stay in bed. The girl hadn't been too well lately, not since the night of the Hospital Ball, in fact. She'd been off-colour. Not herself. A little more irritable and impatient with him than usual. And that, when he came to think of it, was admitting a lot.

Diana's attitude to her father was always one of impatient tolerance. He couldn't think why. Hadn't he given her everything she'd ever wanted? What more could a man do to win his daughter's love?

The thought pulled him up abruptly. Was it necessary for him to win his daughter's love? Did he have to buy it? Wasn't it there as naturally and spontaneously as his love for her? If not, there was something radically wrong somewhere.

In a rare moment of self-criticism Joseph Langdon wondered whether he had deluded himself all these years in believing that his daughter held him in as deep affection as he held her. Had he over-indulged her? Been too lavish, too generous, not only with his money, but with his adoration?

But she was his whole world, it was for her that he worked. For her he had built up his financial kingdom and a fortune which one day she would inherit. There was no limit to his ambitions for her. With all her advantages she could easily marry a title—and not an impecunious one either.

Therefore he was troubled because her time and attention seemed to be taken up with that village doctor. A nice fellow in his way, but unambitious. Joseph had held Christopher in veiled contempt ever since the young man had confessed that he had no desire to reach Harley Street.

'I'm a village doctor,' he'd said once, 'and like being a village doctor. I can do as good a job here as anywhere else—a more worthwhile one, too. I'd rather treat peope who were genuinely ill than bored society women with nothing better to do with their time than indulge in imaginary ailments.'

'But it's your job to treat 'em, lad. No matter what's wrong with them—or what they imagine's wrong with 'em. The question is, who's got the brass. I should have thought that you, as a Yorkshireman, would have known that.'

Joseph dismissed the thought of Christopher Maynard and departed for church after extracting a promise from Diana that she wouldn't get up before lunch.

'And if you're no better tomorrow, my girl, we'd better have the doctor to look at you.'

But that meant Christopher Maynard, so he added hastily: 'And I don't mean the local

226

doctor, either. I'll get Sir James Holford over from Falmouth to give you a proper check-up.'

'Christopher could do that,' she answered pettishly. 'He's a fully qualified doctor, and a good one, too.'

'Ay, so I've heard tell, but not experienced enough.'

'He was experienced enough to be appointed in Doctor Peterson's place,' Diana pointed out hastily.

Joseph had no answer to that.

And so he departed for church none too easy in his mind. Diana was always too swift in her defence of young Doctor Maynard. He was a nice enough fellow, in his way, but not good enough for the daughter of Joseph Langdon—not rich enough, not well-connected enough, and not ambitious enough. A man either had to have a background or brains. The right background meant a title and all that went with it—all, in fact, that he desired for Diana, for which he had educated her and spent money upon her. A man could get along without the right background well enough, if he used his brains in the right way, but no one could say young Doctor Maynard was doing that, Joseph thought aggressively, if he aimed to spend his life doctoring the people in Tresanton.

So when his own luxurious car swept past Christopher's shabby one, Joseph pretended not to see it. But it was difficult not to acknowledge the fellow when his ancient little vehicle was forced to pull into the hedge to allow him to pass. One had, at least, to give him a gracious nod of acknowledgement and thanks.

Christopher smiled to himself as the great Joseph Langdon swept by. So he was on his way to church and Diana wasn't with him. That was all to the good because after he had called upon old Pete Trewin, at the top of the hill, he could continue on his way to The Towers and talk to her without interruption.

Diana, who had been lolling in bed reading the Sunday papers, rose with alacrity when she heard Christopher had called. He'd promised to get in touch with her when they said good night after the dance but he hadn't kept his promise. The trouble with being Tresanton's only doctor was that he was constantly busy— as well she knew—so his neglect of her could only be due to work.

The day would come when all that was at an end, when he would be successful enough to delegate work to other people; when he would no longer be a small-time village doctor, but a well-known Harley Street name; when she need no longer be embarrassed by her father's broad Yorkshire dialect and his uncouth manners. She would see very little of him once they lived in London, and even when they came to Creek House, during the summer months they would spend all their time with the sailing fraternity and an occasional duty visit to her father would suffice.

Diana was still convinced that one day she would acquire Creek House and that she would turn it into a charming country home suitable for an eminent doctor and his wife. Sally wouldn't be able to maintain it for ever unless, of course, she did marry Martin and they made it their home, but that was a contingency Diana refused to contemplate— and not one that was likely to arise if Martin continued to make as poor headway with Sally as he appeared to be doing right now.

What a tiresome pair they were! Diana thought as she touched up her make-up and ran a comb through her smooth blonde hair. Sally had been a vague stumbling block in her path for too long and it was about time she was removed from it finally and irrevocably.

Diana didn't in the least regret the lie she had told about this weekend. All that mattered was that Sally had believed her and to lend emphasis to her story, she had taken the precaution of not appearing in church this morning. Indeed, she had kept carefully out of sight the whole weekend. She'd tried to coax Christopher into spending Saturday and Sunday with her, but had failed. He had an engagement in Falmouth on the Saturday, which was all to the good, and on Sunday he was staying at home to catch up with his deskwork, he'd said. So that meant that Sally was unlikely to see him in Tresanton.

Her father's appearance without her this morning would confirm her own absence, and since no one bothered to talk to him very much no one was likely to ask where his daughter was. Especially Sally. And if she were sitting in the Penfold pew with Martin and his parents, as she usually did, they would leave the church by the west porch, whereas her father never failed to use the main entrance so that everyone could see him arrive and depart.

Supremely confident, therefore, Diana went downstairs to meet Christopher. She went to him with hands outstretched, put her arms about his neck, and kissed him upon the lips. But he didn't respond. She felt the unyielding strength of him and was disturbed by it. She drew back a little and regarded him inquiringly.

'What's the matter?' she chided gently. 'Is it too early in the day for passion?'

He released her hands from his neck and said: 'I want to talk to you, Diana.'

She pouted prettily.

'The other night you wanted to make love to me, Christopher. You were impatient for everyone to be gone. You asked me to curtail the evening so that we could be alone together. Remember? And when I did you brought me home, said good night, and went on your way. Why?'

'Because the evening ended later than I

thought it would. I was tired and had to be up early the next morning, if you remember.'

She let this go and said instead: 'I haven't seen you since the dance, Christopher.'

'I've been busy.'

He was polite, firm, and distant. That annoyed her. She drew away, assuming indifference and hoping, in that way, to provoke him. In her experience the one sure way of arousing a man's desire was to pretend she didn't want him.

'Would you care for a drink?' she said casually.

'No thank you, Diana.'

She regarded him with a teasing little smile.

'You don't want to make love, you don't want a drink—then what *do* you want?'

'It's half past eleven on a fine Sunday morning and I'm in the mood for conversation, Diana.'

'Then start it,' she commanded prettily.

He asked abruptly: 'Why did you tell Sally you were going to Yorkshire this weekend to meet my aunt?'

Her baby-blue eyes opened wide in astonishment.

'Darling, what *are* you talking about?'

'You heard, Diana, and I'm waiting for your answer.'

'How can I answer when I don't understand the question?'

'Then I'll put it to you a little more clearly.

You told Sally I was taking you to Yorkshire this weekend to meet my aunt. That was a lie and I want to know why you told it.'

Her laughter tinkled in astonishment.

'Sally told you I said *that*? Then it was she who was lying, Christopher, not I.'

Her regarded her carefully for a long moment. She had never looked so lovely—but he always thought that when he was with her. The strange thing was that she was so easy to forget once out of sight. But Sally Peterson wasn't. She hadn't half this girl's beauty, and yet she was ten times more alive to him. It was true that he wanted to make love to Diana the other night—and not for the first time, either. She was the kind of girl many men would want to make love to—physically, at any rate. But that was the trouble with Diana. Her appeal was entirely physical. There was nothing beyond it—nothing mentally stimulating, or spiritually satisfying. She was a creature of the flesh and the charms of the flesh didn't last for ever, whereas Sally's warmth and sincerity would be undying.

Diana said briskly: 'Just when did Sally tell you this?'

'On Saturday.'

'Saturday!' she said on a quick little breath. 'I thought you were going to Falmouth on Saturday?'

'So I did. I saw her after I got back.'

'And yet you refused to come here to dine

with me,' she reproached.

'We met by accident. She was at the Blundells' cottage and I happened to drop in.'

Diana said, with a faintly disapproving air: 'I can't understand Sally's friendship with that couple.'

'She likes them,' Christopher said abruptly. 'So do I. She met Stella Blundell when I sent the girl along to the hospital for an X-ray. Sally's been interested in her case ever since.'

'Indeed!' Diana's pencilled eyebrows lifted in faint surprise. 'Has she any right to be interested in your cases? I thought she was a house-physician at the hospital. Surely her activities should be confined there?'

'It's lucky for me, and for Stella, that she happened to be available on Saturday,' Christopher said briskly. 'Otherwise I might have lost my patient and Stella would certainly have lost her baby.'

For a brief moment Diana was very still, then she asked slowly: 'Do you mean to tell me she actually attended a patient of yours?'

'Believing I was away in Yorkshire, she did the humane thing and helped in an emergency. Young Mrs. Blundell's child was born prematurely as the result of a fall. It was lucky Sally was around.'

'But *you* are Mrs. Blundell's doctor. I don't think the Medical Board, or the Hospital Board, for that matter, would view Sally's intervention with such charity.'

233

'Neither the Medical Board nor the Hospital Board are going to know anything about it. And even if they did, the explanation is simple enough. Thanks to you, Sally believed I was hundreds of miles away.'

Diana made an impatient gesture. 'Don't be so stupid, Christopher—or so gullible! She obviously told you that story to excuse her own actions. Don't you realise she's never forgiven you for stepping into her father's shoes? She came home firmly believing she would be appointed to the practice. And what happened? You were, instead; and she's resented you ever since. Her only reason for being so friendly with the Blundells was that she saw an opportunity of ingratiating herself with one of your patients. And if you weren't so trusting you'd have seen that.'

Christopher hadn't thought it possible that he could be so angry. For a moment he looked at Diana in stunned astonishment—astonished to discover that she could be so malicious, she whom he had always believed to be as sweet as she was lovely.

'What's the matter?' she asked curiously. 'Why are you looking at me like that?'

'Perhaps I'm seeing you for the first time, Diana.'

'What do you mean?'

Christopher shrugged. 'It doesn't matter. But I thought Sally was your friend—or so you once told me.'

'We were friends from habit, nothing more. We grew up together, and went to school together until I went to France. We were the same age and there was a dearth of young people in Tresanton. I had to take what companionship I could during the holidays.'

'Then you were lucky to find a companion like Sally.'

'Or she was lucky to find me,' Diana retorted.

She wasn't troubling to hide her anger now. She hated Sally, but had never realised how much until this moment. Her attitude towards her had always been one of rather patronising affection, but, underlying it, she had been aware that in some indefinable way, Sally was a challenge. Her very simplicity, her lack of affection, her ordinary clothes, her unspectacular appearance—all, obscurely, were a challenge. She was a challenge because she 'belonged' where Diana did not. She was accepted in this village, her roots were here. People liked her—even loved her—because she was the daughter of old Doc Peterson, one of the long line of Petersons who had been village doctors here for four generations. She hadn't much money, but she didn't need it. She had friends instead—things which Joseph's wealth had never been able to buy either for himself or his daughter, and now, on top of everything, she seemed to have stolen Christopher's esteem. But not more than that,

235

Diana thought frantically. *Surely* not more than that?

A swift and unfamiliar panic touched Diana's heart. Her supreme self-confidence was briefly shaken. She was afraid and she, who had never known fear, didn't like it. She wanted to go to Christopher and implore him not to desert her. Her anxiety was almost humbling, and she hated it. No man had ever humbled her before. So why should this village doctor? What was it about him that made him so important? There had been plenty of men in her life, but none had mattered so much as he.

His attraction, she acknowledged frankly, was more than merely biological. His character appealed to her as well as his looks and strength and virility. He was a dedicated man—dedicated to his work. And oh, she thought passionately, how I could help him!, With me as his wife he could reach the top of his profession. He wouldn't have to remain buried alive in a little Cornish village!

She said falteringly: 'Christopher, can't we forget all this? After all, it isn't important. Sally can do her damnedest to take your patients from you, and make up all the stories she likes, but we don't have to care. You can afford to ignore them. You're a fine doctor and you'll go far.'

'Go far?' he echoed. 'I'm quite content where I am.'

236

'But not for always!' she protested. 'I know you're fond of Tresanton—so am I, for that matter—but there are bigger fields to conquer than these.'

Christopher laughed.

'I'm not the conquering type, Diana.'

'Oh, but you are! You conquered me from the moment we met.'

He was suddenly embarrassed. He hadn't intended that the conversation should take such a personal turn. And even now he hadn't obtained the answer he had come for—she hadn't admitted that she lied to Sally. But what did it matter? He knew which of the two girls he believed.

All of a sudden his own personal feelings were straightened out. He saw things in perspective, at last—even Diana's attraction for him, which he had been on the brink of mistaking for love. It was as if a spotlight was suddenly focused upon all that was real and important to him.

Diana had a sudden sense of defeat. He had turned his back upon her. He was going. He didn't even seem to have heard her last remark.

She said quickly: 'Christopher, don't go!'

'I'm sorry,' he said, 'I've one or two calls to make. And your father will be home from church soon. He won't be over-pleased to find me here.'

'You don't give him a chance to know you,

237

or understand you, as I do.'

'He's a busy man,' Christopher answered lightly. 'We're both busy men.'

'Christopher, I'm trying to *tell* you something!'

He regarded her with a strange compassion and answered gently: 'Don't tell me, Diana. I don't want to hear it.'

CHAPTER NINETEEN

The offices of Messrs. Penfold, Penfold and Penfold had been situated in the High Street for more than fifty years—and it was about time they dug themselves out of it, thought Diana as she walked through the old-fashioned entrance on Monday morning. But it was all so typical of Martin! He was deep-dyed in tradition and if he ever had any sons they would undoubtedly follow in his footsteps, clinging to the same out-worn ideals, living their lives amidst musty old files and deed-boxes. And absolutely content to do so.

A small town solicitor—that was all Martin would ever be. The firm, which had been founded by his grandfather, had jogged along for three generations, making a very comfortable living. And, of course, since her father had put his affairs in their hands they had been on to a very good thing. Diana wondered if Penfold, Penfold and Penfold had realised just how good a thing, in those long-ago days when her father, a rough, uneducated northerner—had arrived in this village with an eye to the main chance—the main chance being the neglected china clay buried in its forgotten earth. Now he was their biggest and, therefore, their most important client—which was Martin's reason for dropping everything at a moment's notice in order to receive the daughter of that important client.

The moment Joseph had left for his office that morning, Diana had telephone Martin immediately.

'I've got to see you, Martin. It's important.'

It had been more of a command than a request and, as she expected, Martin had been eager to please.

'I'll come to The Towers any time you wish,' he said.

'No, not here. I'll see you in your office. And make it early—I've a hairdresser's appointment at eleven.'

So here she was, almost before the day's routine had begun, climbing the narrow flight of stairs and wondering why solicitor's offices always seemed like relics from the past. Half-way up the stairs there was a little landing where the steps spiralled. A woman was plodding laboriously down them and, on reaching the curve in the stairs, stepped aside respectfully to allow Diana to pass. Diana scarcely glanced at her, vaguely aware that it was the familiar figure of one of the village women—Cruwys was the name, wasn't it?— who obliged in all sorts of capacities throughout the village, augmenting her meagre widow's pension with odd jobs.

The woman glanced at Diana and received in return a patronising little nod. Diana was scarcely aware of her, but old Mrs. Cruwys watched the retreating figure with speculative interest. She was always interested in the goings-on of the local inhabitants, for her own life was narrow and lonely. And she was specially interested in the glamorous Miss Langdon, who had always seemed to her like a princess from a story book—but a disappointing princess, thought old Mrs. Cruwys as she laboured downstairs. There was no warmth, no kindness about her. She was cold all through and it seemed a pity that that nice Doctor Maynard was getting himself tied up with a girl like her.

When Diana saw Martin in his book-lined office she thought spontaneously how absolutely right he looked. The heavy mahogany furniture, the thick faded carpets, even the enormous volumes of legal history behind their plate-glass doors, all contributed to a perfect background for him. And he wore the inevitable black jacket, stiff white collar and pin-stripe trousers. He looked every inch the solicitor. But he had greater dignity and authority than usual. She was seeing another side of him, the real side of him, and it pleased her because it gave her confidence in him. Here was a man who would see that justice was done—and that was what she wanted.

He was courteous and charming, with the reassuring air which seemed to come automatically to the legal mind. He installed her in a comfortable arm-chair, with cigarettes at her elbow, and even inquired, solicitously, whether she would care for a cup of coffee.

She brushed all this aside impatiently. 'I've very little time, Martin.'

Instantly he was attentive, business-like and deferential—but not over-deferential.

She came to the point at once. 'Martin, I'm worried about Sally.'

This surprised him. He had thought of all sorts of reasons for her visit, none of which included Sally. He had even had her long metal deed-box brought up from the strong room, and there it was on the desk before him, with her name written in immaculate copperplate on a small white card.

She looked at it and smiled briefly. 'You can put that away. It isn't my personal affairs I've come to see you about.'

'So I gather,' he answered in surprise. 'Why are you worried about Sally?'

She leaned forward with a sense of urgency. 'Martin, you know how she'd set her heart upon acquiring her father's practice when he died?'

A rueful smile touched Martin's lips. 'I should say I do. There isn't much about Sally that I don't know.'

'Oh, but there is! And I'm perfectly sure that if you knew what she was doing now you would want to stop her.' His brows met in a swift and questioning frown. 'What do you mean?' he asked.

'Simply that she's been indulging in unethical, and I'm not sure if it isn't illegal, behaviour.'

Martin was so astonished that he dropped his professional air. 'What the devil do you mean?' he demanded.

'Simply that she is attending patients whom she has no right to attend. Doctor Maynard's, in fact.'

'I don't believe it!'

'I didn't believe it myself, at first, but it's true, Martin. That's why I'm worried about her. She could get into serious trouble for this sort of behaviour. She could be dismissed from the hospital and I'm not so sure that she couldn't be crossed off the medical register. Of course,' Diana added, thoughtfully studying Martin's worried face, 'you might not be sorry about that.'

'Well, of course I should,' he protested.

'But why? If she were forced to give up medicine, you'd have no further trouble in persuading her to marry you, I'm sure.'

'What makes you think I'm having trouble?' he asked stiffly.

'Because if you weren't you'd have married her by now.'

How shrewd she was, he thought in astonishment. Almost as shrewd as that father of hers. Why had he believed her to be merely beautiful and nothing more? He was a little embarrassed by her perception. She saw too much, but what she saw was true, all the same. And what she said was true, also, at least as far as his relationship with Sally was concerned.

He said slowly: 'Don't you think you'd better be more frank, Diana? These accusations you're making against Sally—'

She interrupted swiftly: 'But I'm not accusing her! And I'm certainly not against her. That's why I've come to you. We're both her friends, Martin. We must help her— *you* must help her.'

'How can I until I hear what's she's been doing?'

'But I've told you!'

'Only that she's been attending patients of Doctor Maynard's. Which patients, and in what circumstances? I'll have to have all the details.'

'I'll tell you all I know,' Diana said confidentially, 'and please believe that I'm here only as Sally's friend. You know I've always had her welfare at heart. You had evidence of that when she came home for her father's funeral, remember?'

He remembered only too well his brief interview with Diana at The Towers and the sudden understanding that had leapt between them, the surprise he had felt at realising that Diana was genuinely concerned for himself and Sally. He'd always been shy of her until that moment, even a little afraid, but she had revealed herself as his ally.

He had to remember that now and forget that it was she, and she alone, who had exposed him to that embarrassing moment at the dance. He had bitterly resented her because of that, but worse had followed. Sally's rejection of him was the most bitter pill of all. Even now he couldn't really believe it. He was ready to forgive and forget, to regard the whole scene indulgently, to treat it as the whim of a girl hesitating on the brink of marriage. Women behaved in extraordinary ways sometimes and a man had to be patient and understanding. Sally's mood that night had been a sort of stage-fright, nothing more, he assured himself, and although he had felt angry on his way home he had still felt confident that she would come to her senses.

Diana was waiting for him to speak—a little impatiently, he thought—but he could say nothing. He was too dumbfounded and worried. He didn't want Sally involved in any trouble. Nothing shocked his conventional mind more than the thought of scandal, so, although he wanted Sally to give up medicine, he wanted her to do so voluntarily—not because her name was smeared in glaring headlines across the pages of the local newspapers. Although, he thought magnanimously, it wouldn't make any difference to his love for her, he would marry her just the same. But she would certainly be more acceptable with an unbesmirched name.

'Will you come to the point, Diana?'

'All right. On Saturday she delivered a baby that she had no right to deliver. The patient was Christopher's.'

Martin looked astonished, but there was more than that behind his swift and questioning glance.

'Oh no,' she said, interpreting correctly, 'I'm not concerned for Christopher, only for Sally. He's a fine doctor; he can hold his own.'

'Against what?' Martin asked involuntarily.

'Against Sally's determination to get the practice back from him.'

'Oh, come now!' he protested.

'But it's true, Martin. Sally is obsessed with the idea. She always has been. She's never forgiven Christopher for being appointed in her place.'

'I find that hard to believe, Diana. It seemed to me, the other night, that they were very good friends.'

Diana brushed that aside. 'A cover-up—no more. She's had to accept him and she's had to do so, on the surface, with good grace. Inwardly, she still feels the same way about him.'

She couldn't understand the extraordinary look of relief which crossed Martin's face.

'Go on,' he said briskly. 'I'm listening.'

'The patient is the wife of one of my father's pit workers. She had a fall on Saturday and he ran to fetch Christopher. On the way he met Sally, and she told him that Christopher was away and that *she* would attend to his wife.'

'Then that explains it,' Martin said reasonably.

'But Christopher wasn't away.'

'Then, for some reason, Sally obviously believed he was.'

'But she didn't trouble to find out. She didn't even telephone his house. Christopher has a woman who goes in daily and when she's not there the people next door take messages. So you see, there was no reason in the world why Sally couldn't have got in touch with him wherever he was—except that she didn't want to.'

Martin said slowly: 'This is a pretty serious thing.'

'Of course it's serious! That's why I'm here. Sally saw the chance to take one of his patients and seized it.'

'But she couldn't actually take his patients from him,' Martin pointed out immediately.

'No, but she could win their confidence.

246

Nearly everyone in this village was a patient of her father's. Bit by bit, she could turn them against Christopher, and once a doctor lost the confidence of his patients, he'd just have to give up, wouldn't he?'

But Martin was still unconvinced.

'It seems to me,' he said slowly, 'that your concern is really for Christopher.'

Diana shrugged. 'You can believe that if you like, but if it were would I come to you? Christopher can look after himself. He doesn't need anyone's help. But Sally does.' She gave him one of her winning and confidential smiles. 'Please believe me, Martin.'

He did believe her—how could he fail to? What she said was the simple truth. If her desire was not to help Sally she need do nothing at all in the matter, much less appeal to him.

She continued briskly: 'I saw Jim Blundell, that's the father of the baby, on my way here this morning. He'd been to the hospital to see his wife. The mother and child were moved there the day after the birth so he was a little late going on duty. He told me how he'd met Sally on Saturday and how grateful he was to her. Naturally, when he believed his wife's own doctor was away!'

'If Sally believed that, too, she acted in what she thought to be an emergency.'

'But the Hospital Board wouldn't see it that way, would they? Or the Medical Council?

They would consider her guilty of unprofessional conduct, and you know it. Your father's on the Hospital Board, isn't he?' she added negligently.

'As legal adviser, yes.'

'And you know the Medical Superintendent well?'

'Very well,' Martin admitted. 'We play golf together.'

'I thought so . . .'

'But you don't imagine, do you, that I'd tell him about all this?'

'It wouldn't be a matter of telling tales, Martin, and I honestly think it would be a better way than speaking to Sally about it. You know how stubborn she is.'

He knew that well enough.

Diana continued urgently: 'At all costs, you mustn't antagonise her, Martin, but if you remonstrate with her you certainly will, no matter how tactfully you do it. I know Sally of old. She's as stubborn as a mule.'

'Then what do you suggest I do?' he asked.

She wanted to point out that he was the solicitor, not she, and then remembered that she had not come for his legal aid, but in his capacity as a friend.

'The Medical Superintendent thinks quite highly of Sally, doesn't he?'

'I believe so,' Martin acknowledged.

'Then he wouldn't want her to get into any sort of professional trouble—and he wouldn't want his own hospital staff to involve him in any censure. So surely the best thing is to have a tactful word with him? Tell him, if you like, that Sally really did think she was acting in an emergency—although I'm perfectly convinced she didn't. Her aim is to get her father's practice again. She is obsessed with the idea, but it's nothing more than a whim. She still feels that she has to fulfil her father's ambitions. She was only too conscious of them when we were at school together, but I don't really think her heart was set on being a doctor. She just thought that she owed it to her father—that there had to be another Doctor Peterson to carry on the family tradition. Well, that sort of thing is all right for a man, but not for a girl. Sally ought to marry and settle down.'

Martin couldn't have agreed with Diana more. He himself had expressed these very sentiments to Sally at the time of her father's death, but she had stubbornly declared her intention to fulfil her father's dreams.

So everything Diana said was true. She was right in every way.

'All the same,' he said reluctantly, 'I don't like the idea of reporting her to the Medical Superintendent.'

Diana shrugged.

'That's up to you. But it wouldn't be a question of *reporting* her. All you need do is show your concern for her. And if the Medical

Superintendent took a dim view of the whole affair and dismissed her, would it really matter? She'd get over it eventually. In fact, she'd get over it very quickly once she married you. But as long as she has this bee in her bonnet about being a doctor, I doubt if she ever *will* marry you, Martin.'

He looked away, unwilling to reveal that Sally had already rejected him.

It was almost as if Diana were throwing him a lifeline, but it was a line he had to grasp and handle very carefully. Certainly the most effective way of bringing Sally to her senses would be for her to lose her job. And after all, a mere house-physician wasn't so important. She was by no means irreplaceable.

'Personally,' Diana said as she picked up her gloves and handbag and prepared to go, 'I don't think for a minute that the Medical Super. would clamp down heavily upon her unless, of course, she continued to do this sort of thing. That's why she's got to be stopped, right now. You'd be acting in her own interests, Martin. You'd have nothing to feel guilty about.'

She held out her hand and gave him a vivid smile. 'Don't worry,' she said, 'I've every confidence in you. In fact, I don't know anyone who'd handle a situation like this as ably as you.'

The words bolstered his self-esteem and helped to eliminate any lingering doubt or fear. Of course, she was right. At first her suggestion had seemed a little astonishing, even a little underhand, but, as she said, it was just a question of tact and he prided himself that he had plenty of that.

Diana was also right when she said that the wrong line of attack would be to reproach Sally. She was a stubborn little goose, and she was certainly behaving very foolishly. She couldn't hope to win back her father's practice by such devious means, but tell her that and she'd be up in arms. No, he decided, Diana's method was by far the best. A discreet word to the Medical Superintendent would do no harm. It might even do a lot of good, and he hoped that the good would work out on his own side.

CHAPTER TWENTY

Sally was on duty in the Casualty Ward when the summons from the superintendent's office came through. She made a mental survey of her day's work, but could think of nothing amiss. So whatever was behind this summons, she thought with relief, it couldn't be trouble.

But one glance at the super's face told her the reverse. Doctor Armstrong was a fair-minded man and for many years had been a personal friend of her father's. But he didn't smile when she came in.

'Sit down, Sally. I want to have a talk with you.'

In the course of duty he was not a lenient man, but he was a tolerant and understanding chief, a fine doctor, and a good man to work for. He was sympathetic and humane. His smile, though rare, was sincere—but he had no smile for her now.

She read concern in his eyes, and a little lurch of fear stirred her heart. Something had gone wrong, something serious, otherwise she would not have been called to this holy of holies. She came under the direct supervision of the Chief Resident Physician, so any misdemeanour was his province. Then what was wrong? Sally wondered with a touch of panic, and groped about in her mind for a clue. There was none. All she could do was to sit there and wait for Doctor Armstrong to speak.

For a moment he stared at some papers on his desk, frowning a little, but somehow she knew his concentration was not upon his work, but upon her offence—whatever it was.

He said suddenly: 'A serious matter has been brought to my attention, Doctor Peterson, and it concerns yourself.'

He looked at her taut young figure. She was sitting erect in her chair, her hands clasped in her lap. She was apprehensive and a little afraid, but puzzled, too. He sensed her bewilderment and that surprised him, for if she had any sense of guilt she would know why she was here.

She said nothing; just waited. He moved uncomfortably, for he was not enjoying this moment. Sally Peterson was a promising young doctor and, besides, she was the daughter of a man whom he had always admired and respected. Nevertheless, he knew how bitterly disappointed she had been when another man acquired her father's practice. Could that *really* be the reason, as Martin Penfold suggested, for doing what she had done?

He cleared his throat and came directly to the point.

'It has been brought to my notice that you attended a patient outside the precincts of this hospital—a patient whom you have no right to attend.'

Sally's face went pale. So that's it, she thought. Someone had told him about Stella Blundell's baby.

'If you mean the emergency delivery last Saturday night, sir—'

'I do.'

Sally experienced a little rush of relief. 'But I can explain that!'

'I shall be glad if you can.'

'It was an emergency, sir. Mrs. Blundell had a fall—a serious one. I met her husband when he was on his way to fetch Doctor Maynard.'

'I have heard that,' the superintendent

253

interrupted.

'Well, then—' Sally made a little gesture with her hands, a gesture of inquiry, as if it were she, not he, who required an explanation.

'Emergency or no emergency,' said the superintendent, 'you acted unprofessionally. I suppose you are aware of that?'

'I wasn't at the time, sir. It did occur to me later—yes.'

'But it didn't occur to you to fetch the patient's own doctor? I understand she's registered with Doctor Maynard under the National Health Service.'

'That's true, sir. But he was away—or I thought he was.'

'You didn't even try to get a message to him?'

'I didn't think it possible, sir. I believed him to be hundreds of miles away.'

Doctor Armstrong looked at her in surprise and, she felt, with a touch of hope, as if he were wanting her to convince him of her innocence.

'I understand that when you met young Mr. Blundell you told him to go no farther and that you, yourself, would attend to his wife.'

'Yes—' Sally faltered. 'I thought, in the circumstances, it was the only thing to do.'

Doctor Armstrong leaned his elbows upon his desk and said urgently: 'I didn't want to believe this story, I don't want to believe it now, whatever your motive for acting the way

254

you did.'

Sally interrupted indignantly: 'Motive, sir? What motive could I have but to help the patient?'

'That, I'm afraid, is not what many people in Tresanton will think—nor the Hospital Board, should they hear of it.'

A chill of fear ran like an icy finger down Sally's spine.

'I don't understand, sir.'

'Don't you? I see I shall have to be more frank. In a community like this no one's private affairs remain private for very long. Your reaction to Doctor Maynard's appointment was well known—and understandable, no doubt. But in rushing off to attend a patient of his in so unorthodox a fashion, the worst possible interpretation could be put upon it.'

Sally stared at him aghast. 'What interpretation?' she stammered.

Doctor Armstrong answered gently: 'The malicious might say that you hoped to win Doctor Maynard's patients from him.'

'But that's absurd, sir! I couldn't do such a thing.'

'I know that, but gossip is gossip and, in a small community like this, a dangerous thing. The hospital can't afford to be exposed to it. *You*, as a doctor, can't afford to be exposed to it.'

Sally's mouth was suddenly dry. She tried to speak, but words would not come.

Doctor Armstrong continued: 'Do you understand what I mean, Sally?'

'You mean—I'm to be dismissed?' Her voice sounded shrill and taut in her own ears, but to Doctor Armstrong it sounded merely pitiable. His heart was moved with concern for her.

'There is an alternative,' he said kindly, 'and one I would personally prefer. You could tender your resignation.'

Her whole body seemed to slump.

'Believe me,' he said swiftly, 'I don't want it. You're a promising young doctor and you have a future before you. That is why I don't want it spoilt by slander and gossip, but by now the story is probably all over the village and even beyond. I can't keep it from the ears of the Hospital Board. That is why I've sent for you now, before they demand an inquiry.' He saw that her slim young hands were clutching the sides of her chair, the knuckles showing white. He wanted desperately to help her and continued urgently: 'I'm thinking of your future, Sally. I don't want it jeopardised. If you're dismissed from this hospital for unprofessional conduct—and you can be— you'll find it difficult to get another job.'

That, she thought in a remote part of her mind, was an understatement.

'But if you resign,' Doctor Armstrong continued, 'you can state that your reason is because you want to better yourself and that

256

there is little chance of advancement here. I'll confirm that and give you the highest possible reference. Then, later, when it has all blown over and been forgotten, I'll find an opening for you, should you want to return. Don't you realise,' he said anxiously, 'that what I want to do is to *help* you? When the Board demands an inquiry I want to be able to say that there is nothing to inquire into, because the doctor concerned is no longer on my staff. That is the only way in which the matter can be dropped.'

Sally said piteously: 'But I don't want to leave this way! Besides, I think it unfair. I acted in all good faith, believing that what I did was the right thing to do. And when Doctor Maynard came along, he didn't reproach me. He said he was glad of my help.'

Doctor Armstrong made no answer. There was little he could say. Besides, he was surprised to learn that Doctor Maynard had been there. This was a fact Martin Penfold had omitted.

He hadn't wanted to believe Penfold's story at all—but then, he'd never liked the fellow very much. He was too pompous, too self-satisfied, too virtuous altogether. But when he'd said: 'I want to talk to you, Doctor Armstrong. I'm worried about Sally,' what could he do but listen? And in all fairness it had to be admitted that Martin had acted purely out of concern for the girl he wanted to marry—not, the Medical Superintendent thought wryly, that he seemed to have had much success in that direction so far, and he couldn't see that telling tales behind her back was going to advance the fellow's case. But, all things aside, the professional behaviour of one of his staff was a matter of deep concern to him and after long thought he had decided that the only possible solution was to ask for Sally's resignation.

And besides, he thought tiredly, the fact that Doctor Maynard *had* turned up didn't exactly ease the situation. The fact remained that a doctor on the hospital staff had attended his patient, without the authority to do so, and without trying to contact him, so Maynard had every justification to report the matter, if he wished, to the local Medical Council.

Doctor Armstrong wanted to believe that Sally's behaviour had been prompted only by concern for the patient, and not by any ulterior motive, such as Martin Penfold suggested. 'She's got a bee in her bonnet about that practice of her father's,' he had said, 'and I think she may have some foolish idea that she can win it back. She's young and impulsive, you know.' His indulgent tone had infuriated Doctor Armstrong—infuriated him so much that he'd refused to listen any further. He'd heard the facts of the case, confirmed apparently by the father of the child, who was enthusiastic in his praise of young Doctor

Peterson's help and skill. No doubt the young fellow had spread it all over the village by now—certainly at the chalk pit where he worked—so it wouldn't be very long before the whole place was buzzing with it. The hospital too. And once the news spread about the hospital it wouldn't be long before the Board of Governors was asking the Medical Superintendent for an explanation.

He sighed and ran a hand through his grey hair, saying yet again: 'I'm sorry, Sally. Really sorry. But I know the hospital where you trained wanted you back. You'll be happy there, I'm sure.'

She rose stiffly and crossed to the door. Her movements were almost mechanical, as if outside her own volition. Suddenly she turned.

'There is just one thing I would like to know, sir, and that is the name of your informant.'

He had hoped she wouldn't ask that, for he had given his word not to mention Penfold's name. At the time Martin's request had seemed a little odd for surely, he'd thought, if the fellow could come to me with the story, he could face her with it? But then Martin had hurriedly explained: 'I'd rather she wasn't aware that I know anything about it. The less people who do know, the better, I think. That's why I've come to you—not to punish her, but to help her. She probably doesn't realise what a serious thing she's done, or what it could mean. Can't we spare her, somehow? If she were to leave the hospital, for instance, if she were no longer a member of the staff, she couldn't be punished by hospital discipline, could she?'

It had seemed the only solution, even a good and practical one, for at least it wouldn't put a brake upon her career. She could start again elsewhere.

'Who was it, sir?' Sally asked again, urgently.

Doctor Armstrong jerked back to the moment.

'Someone who was concerned about the matter, my dear. Let's leave it at that, shall we?'

She could see that he meant to, that she wouldn't find out from him the identity of his informant.

But did she need to? she thought bitterly as she left the room. There was only one person with the right to complain. Christopher himself.

She walked blindly along the corridor, feeling as if the bottom had dropped out of her world. Not so much because she was to leave the hospital, but because she felt betrayed and hurt—hurt by the one man who mattered most of all to her. The man she was deeply and irrevocably in love with.

CHAPTER TWENTY-ONE

The rest of the afternoon passed in a daze. Sally did her work with mechanical precision, but all the time her stunned mind was floundering in a bog of bewilderment; all the time one sickening truth tormented her—that Christopher, despite his praise on Saturday, had suddenly about-faced and betrayed her.

It seemed the only answer, for who else knew of the incident? Only Martha, and she would be the last person to tell Doctor Armstrong. Besides which, she was probably unaware that there had been anything unethical in Sally's behaviour. To her, a doctor was a doctor. She knew nothing of red tape and professional etiquette.

And she had been more than proud when Christopher had said next day: 'Sally was a wonderful help last night, Martha. She's her father's daughter, all right.'

The woman had looked as gratified as a doting mother, nodding her head in complete agreement.

It just didn't make sense, thought Sally in the stunned recesses of her mind. A man wasn't a girl's friend one day and her enemy the next. Especially a man like Christopher. When he had come to Creek House on Sunday he had been gay and smiling, thoroughly

261

enjoying himself, working in the garden with zest and enthusiasm. Between them they had planted a host of daffodil and hyacinth bulbs, narcissi and crocus. 'And if I'm not allowed to feast my eyes on them as often as I wish next spring, I'll consider it a grave injustice!' he had teased.

'You can do more than that,' she promised. 'You can come every day and pick as many as you like, for your house.'

It was then that he had looked at her, gravely and earnestly, as if he had been on the point of saying something vitally important; something intimate and wonderful; something which made a rush of hope beat with urgent wings against her heart.

But he hadn't said it. Nevertheless, she had felt that it was only a postponement, that later she would hear what he had been about to say and her world would be transformed because of it.

She had no reason for such a feeling, nothing definite on which to base it, but it had been a deep and strong awareness, creeping unbidden into her heart.

He had taken her hand abruptly and turned her towards the house. 'There's Martha, calling us in for tea,' he'd said, and the strength of his hand had closed about her fingers, holding them close. Nor did he release them. And so they had walked hand in hand across the lawn, united in a deep contentment.

262

Not until they reached the porch did he let her go—and even then, she felt, unwillingly. He looked down at her and said quietly: 'Thank you for a wonderful afternoon, Sally. I love this house. I love this garden. I love—'

But what else he loved she had never heard, for there was Martha, broad and buxom and beaming, standing arms akimbo and scolding good-naturedly: 'Don't you dare put mud on my nice clean carpets, you two! Leave your shoes out there on the step!' And they had sat down upon the porch seat, side by side, laughing a little like two guilty children, as they obediently kicked off their shoes.

And then suddenly Christopher caught Sally up and carried her over the threshold. 'You can't walk about in stockinged feet,' he had said, his face very close to her own. And before setting her down in the carpeted hall he had held her thus, high against his heart, and an ecstasy such as she had never known swept through her.

The moment had been brief, but beautiful—and surely he had felt it, too? For his face had suddenly been still, no longer smiling, no longer teasing, but tense and serious and flushed, as if a sudden warmth, as disturbing as that which touched her, had engulfed him, too.

He set her down abruptly and she ran upstairs, her heart racing. 'I imagined it!' she thought wildly, but knew that she had not. The magic remained with her as she bathed and changed, choosing her frock with care and finally deciding upon a blue dress which he had admired that weekend when first they met; the last weekend she had spent with her father.

The magic lingered throughout the evening. It was a warm and lovely and tremulous thing, uniting them in rapture. 'And it wasn't only on my side,' she thought with conviction. 'He felt it, too. I'm sure he felt it, too!' That was why he prolonged the evening, until at last Martha came in and said:

'Do you realise what the time is, Doctor? I'd have you know this girl of mine has to be on duty early at that hospital.'

'Marching orders!' he had laughed. 'And I resent them, Sally. I don't want to go.'

Would a man like that turn against her so suddenly? Would he stab her in the back without warning and without reason? She couldn't believe it. Yet there was no other explanation, no other source from which Doctor Armstrough could have obtained his information. Not from Martha, not from Jim Blundell, whose gratitude for Sally's help been touching and sincere.

So the only other person was Christopher. She had to accept that fact, whether she liked it or not.

Before going off duty Sally went into the medical staff common-room and wrote her resignation. It didn't take long, it needed only a few brief lines, but it delayed her sufficiently to miss her bus home. Her father's ancient car had gone in for repair. And when it's ready, she thought now, the best thing I can do is sell it. I'll need the money to get back to London—if St. Mark's will have me.

But she had no doubt they would, if a suitable vacancy was available, for the super. had told her so on leaving. It had pleased her then, but now the thought was depressing, for it meant turning her back upon Tresanton and Creek House and all the things—and the people—she loved most.

Including Christopher.

She shook herself mentally and decided that instead of waiting half an hour for the next bus, she would walk home. A good brisk walk beside the creek would do her good and help to brace her for the moment ahead—the moment when she told Martha what had happened.

She was half-way home when a car swept past her, braked abruptly, and reversed. Sally recognised it as Diana's long, low sports car, and looked about for a means of escape. At this moment Diana was the last person she wished to see.

But there was no escape. Diana's clear voice hailed her. 'Sally, is that you? Where are you going?'

'Home. I've just come off duty.'

'Then jump in, and I'll take you.'

Unwillingly, Sally obeyed. She didn't want to. She felt in no mood for Diana's bright and empty chatter, and as a drift of her expensive perfume filtered across, Sally had an impulse to jump out of the car and continue walking. But it was too late. The engine was in gear, the accelerator throbbing, and they were soaring away through the night, with the creek road unfurling like a ribbon before the powerful headlights.

When they reached Creek House, Sally said politely: 'Won't you come in, Diana?' Not because she wanted to, but because Diana switched off the engine and stepped out of the car, apparently intending to come in, anyway.

The moment Sally entered the softly-lit hall and felt the warmth of her home reach out to enfold her, something inside her seemed to snap. She couldn't go away, she couldn't leave all this! She loved it too much. Her roots were here, her heart was here—and here it would remain, not only because this was where it belonged, but because only recently Christopher had been here—happy and companionable and contented, as if he, too, belonged to Creek House.

She heard Martha's voice saying in concern: 'Why, Sally-love, what's the matter? You're as white as a little ghost!' And then she was in the woman's maternal arms, sobbing out her story incoherently and bitterly, forgetful of Diana.

Martha was aghast. She said indignantly: 'It

266

isn't true! I don't believe it! I don't believe Doctor Armstrong would do a thing like that! And why should he? You did a wonderful job on Saturday and Doctor Maynard said so himself!'

'But not to the super., apparently. Who else, but he, could have reported me?'

'Now that I *don't* believe, my dear. Doctor Chris isn't that kind of a man. Besides, he likes you too much—and *that's* putting it mildly!'

Diana's voice cut into the moment with the sharp precision of a knife.

'What is all this about?' she demanded. 'Am I to understand that you've been dismissed from the hospital, Sally?'

'That she has not!' Martha began indignantly, but Sally, running a tired hand through her hair, said: 'What's the difference? I've handed in my resignation, and that's that.'

'But why, Sally?'

Diana's voice was full of gentle concern.

'Come into the study, and I'll tell you all about it,' Sally suggested.

She didn't know why she chose the study— her father's favourite room—unless it was because she needed him badly at this moment. She found a measure of comfort in the sight of his big desk and leather-covered chair, in his pipe, just as he had left it in the deep ash-tray, in his books and possessions, in the very atmosphere he had breathed.

When Sally closed the door old Martha

267

looked at it for a long moment and then marched firmly to the telephone. It seemed a long time before Christopher answered. She could hear the bell ringing insistently at the other end of the line and its abrupt cessation as he picked up the receiver.

'Maynard here,' he said, and listened in surprise as Martha blurted: 'Doctor, will you come at once, please? It's Miss Sally! She needs you. Badly.'

It didn't take him long to reach Creek House, but another car turned into the drive ahead of him. He recognised it as Martin's neat black saloon, and swore softly beneath his breath. Had Martha sent for him, too? Apparently. That meant she considered Martin's presence essential for Sally's happiness, and his own only essential as a doctor.

But Martha's expression, as she opened the front door to Martin, revealed her surprise.

'I thought you'd be the doctor—' she began, and Martin said swiftly: 'Why? Is Sally ill?'

'Not ill exactly.' She stood aside, reluctantly allowing him to enter, and then her face lit up at the sight of Christopher. 'I'm right glad you've come,' she told him. 'Sally's in her father's study and I'd like a word with you before she comes out—'

'What's the matter?' Martin demanded. 'If Sally isn't ill, why was Doctor Maynard sent for? Why not me?'

'Because it's the Doctor she needs,' Martha retorted bluntly. 'He's the only one who can help her—'

She broke off as the study door opened and Diana's voice floated through.

'Well, I shouldn't break your heart over it, Sally! What does it matter if your job has gone? And why bother to look for another? If you've any sense you'll sell this house—my father will buy it, I know, if I ask him to—and then you must marry Martin. Don't you think you've kept him waiting long enough?'

'Certainly she has kept me waiting long enough,' Martin interposed firmly. 'All right, Diana—you can leave the rest to me.'

'The rest?' Christopher echoed sharply. 'What does that mean? That something I don't know about has gone before?'

Diana whirled round, a slow colour mounting her lovely face—a flush of alarm, thought old Martha shrewdly, feeling an obscure satisfaction at the sight. She had never seen Diana Langdon discomfited before.

At the sound of Christopher's voice the study door widened abruptly and Sally stood there—anger in every taut line of her. Martha was glad of the anger, which she regarded as a much healthier sign than Sally's previous despair.

'Why are *you* here?' Sally demanded of Christopher. 'Have you come to gloat?'

He stared at her in blank astonishment.

269

'What the devil do you mean?'

'Precisely what I say!'

'Then explain it!' he commanded.

'Does it *need* explaining?' she answered furiously. 'You know perfectly well what has happened—thanks to you. No one else could possibly have reported me to Doctor Armstrong!'

She advanced menacingly—the angry, fighting Sally he had come up against once before.

'Let me congratulate you!' she cried. 'Not content with cheating me out of my father's practice, you've now succeeded in hounding me out of the hospital—even out of Tresanton, for what sort of job can I get here now? None, and you know it. Well, I hope you are satisfied, Doctor Maynard!'

She finished on a little sob of fury, standing right in front of him with her dark head thrown back defiantly. He put his hand upon her shoulders and shook her.

'Sally Peterson, I don't know what on earth you are talking about!'

'I don't believe you!'

'You can believe him,' Martin interrupted calmly. 'It was I who spoke to Doctor Armstrong—and for your own good, Sally.'

In the taut little silence which followed Diana said brightly: 'Well, I'll leave you three to settle your little dispute amongst yourselves—' and made for the door.

Christopher's hand shot out and caught her wrist.

'Oh no, you don't, Diana! I've a feeling you're rather essential to it.'

His grip was like a vice. She struggled to free herself, and failed.

'I must go,' she said helplessly. 'I'll be late for dinner and you know how Daddy hates to be kept waiting—'

Even now she managed to put a suggestion of intimacy into her voice, implying—for the benefit of the others and Sally in particular—that Christopher was an intimate part of her life.

'That's too bad, Diana. I'm not letting you go until this mess has been cleared up.'

'*I* have nothing to do with it! If Sally chooses to do things she has no right to do, she has only herself to blame if the hospital asks for her resignation!'

'Have they done that?' Martin asked quickly. 'I'm sorry, Sally, but I thought the most you would get would be a severe reprimand, although I must confess I'm glad if it puts an end to all this career nonsense—'

He broke off, for she was staring at him in a strange and disturbing way, as if she was seeing him for the first time and not liking what she saw.

'Sally, listen to me—'

'I've listened to you quite enough in the past, Martin. I don't intend to, any more.' Her

271

voice had a quiet finality which silenced him.

'But I do,' Christopher said briskly. 'I want to hear just why Penfold talked to Doctor Armstrong, and what he said—*and* who put him up to it.'

His glance flickered to Diana, and a swift rush of fear spread across her lovely face. It was an ugly and evasive fear. She wanted to escape, but Christopher still pinioned her wrist.

'You're hurting me!' she cried.

'But not so much as you wanted to hurt Sally. Why, Diana? Tell me—tell us all—*why*?'

Her mouth set stubbornly.

'Let her go, Christopher,' Sally said. 'And if you don't mind, I'd like you all to go. I want to be alone. But first, I'd like to apologise to you, Christopher. I did you an injustice.'

A fleeting smile touched his mouth.

'You always were impetuous, Sally—but in the present circumstances, I don't blame you. I don't suppose it occurred to you to suspect a man who declared himself to be in love with you, or a woman who pretended to be your friend . . .'

Diana burst out: 'What proof have you—?' and broke off abruptly as, at that precise moment, a woman appeared from the passage leading to the kitchen. Sally recognised her as a village woman who came occasionally to help Martha with household mending, and said automatically: 'Good evening, Mrs. Cruwys.

Are you looking for Martha?'

The woman held a pile of linen in her arms. 'Yes, Miss Sally. I've mended these, but not as well as I'd like to, my rheumatics being so bad. Good evening, Doctor. Good evening, Mr. Penfold, sir. I hope you weren't cross about that ash-tray I broke when I was dusting your desk on Monday morning. I really couldn't help it, sir. Can't grip things, these days, what with my fingers being so twisted, and when you told me to hurry up and finish because Miss Langdon was coming, I got flustered. More haste less speed, as the saying goes!'

'I didn't tell you Miss Langdon was coming!' Martin corrected swiftly.

'But she did come, didn't she, sir? I passed her on the stairs.'

There was an imperceptible moment of silence, and then Diana, ignoring the village woman, drawled: 'And why shouldn't I visit Martin's office? He's my solicitor . . .'

Martha, who had been standing in the hall, took the pile of linen from old Mrs. Cruwys and said: 'Don't you worry about the sewing, Hannah. I know you've done your best.' She added, to Christopher: 'Her rheumatism's been something awful this past week, Doctor.'

She was trying to ease the moment, for there was a sudden tension in the air and whatever was about to explode, thought Martha, had better be delayed until Hannah

273

Cruwys departed, or it would be all over Tresanton by morning.

Christopher said kindly: 'Come to the surgery in the morning, Mrs. Cruwys. You should have come before this—'

'I would've come at the weekend, sir, I was that bad, but knowing you were away, I didn't trouble.'

'Away?' Christopher echoed. 'What made you think I was away?'

'You'd gone to Yorkshire, hadn't you, sir? With Miss Langdon. I heard her telling Miss Sally—'

Diana's voice said shrilly: 'My good woman, what *are* you talking about?'

Hannah Cruwys faltered.

'Why—simply what I say, ma'am.'

'When did you hear Miss Langdon say she was going to Yorkshire with me, Mrs. Cruwys?' Christopher persisted.

The woman looked from one to the other in puzzled surprise.

'The night of the Hospital Ball, sir. I was on duty in the cloakroom and I heard Miss Langdon say—'

'Rubbish!' Diana spat. 'You couldn't have heard a thing! You were asleep!'

A flush of guilt dyed the woman's wrinkled face.

'That's true, ma'am. I shouldn't have dozed off, I suppose, but I *did* wake up. Some coats fell on to my lap—when you took yours, I expect—and that made me come to. That was when I heard you tell Miss Sally you were going to Yorkshire to meet Doctor Maynard's aunt—'

'So Sally did have reason to believe that Christopher was away,' Martin said slowly. 'You didn't tell me any of this, Diana.'

Sally, whose senses were whirling between stunned bewilderment and a wild, unreasoning joy, pulled herself together with an effort.

'Mrs. Cruwys, it's a cold night and you have a long walk home. I'm sure Mr. Penfold won't mind driving you back.'

'Oh, Miss Sally, it's kind of you to think of it! Real kind.' In her rush of pleasure and gratitude the woman forgot her curiosity and the mounting tension in the atmosphere. A tension which had suddenly reached a peak.

Martin said stiffly: 'Of course I'll run you home. Ready, Mrs. Cruwys?'

The little woman shuffled eagerly down the kitchen passage to don her hat and coat.

Martha deliberately mounted the stairs, carrying the mended linen, and the four young people were left alone. Diana, Sally noticed in a detached corner of her mind, was standing very still—standing in a kind of taut misery which ill became her. With a sudden rush of pity for the girl whom she had regarded as her friend, she said tactfully: 'Don't you think it's time we all said good night?'

'Not until I have Martin's assurance that he

will correct the story he took to Doctor Armstrong,' Christopher answered. 'And I'll go with him, to see that he does. I have a lot to say to Armstrong myself. The Hospital Superintendent should know what a fine job you did on Saturday, and how grateful I was for your help. Which, I'd have you know, Penfold, I asked for.'

Sally opened her mouth to contradict and protest, but something in Christopher's glance silenced her. It was a masterful, commanding glance, and beneath it she was silent. Before he went away, Martin turned to Sally.

'I'm sorry—really sorry,' he said. 'But not because I tried to make you marry me—'

She answered: 'Good-bye, Martin.'

'It really is good-bye, isn't it?' he said dully. 'For good?'

'Yes. For good.'

He turned upon his heel and left.

Christopher called after him: 'I'll meet you at the hospital tomorrow at ten!'

Diana suddenly realised that Christopher had let go of her wrist, that he had turned away from her, forgotten her. And she knew with a deep and terrible conviction that she had lost him for ever.

For a long moment she stood looking at his averted back. His attention was all for Sally, as hers was for him.

They've forgotten me, Diana thought numbly. They aren't even aware of me. I don't matter any more, to either of them. I no longer exist . . . .

She turned abruptly and walked out of the house.

As the front door shut heavily behind her, Christopher asked: 'When did you find out that you didn't love Martin?'

'A long time ago.'

'How long ago?'

She hesitated, then said simply: 'Shortly after I met you.'

'And I believed you were going to marry him!'

'I tried to persuade myself to do so.'

'And now?'

She couldn't speak. He put his arm about her shoulders and turned her once again towards her father's study.

'I've something to tell you, Sally, and I'd like to say it in the room your father loved, because he loved you, too . . .'

'Too?' she echoed breathlessly as the door closed behind them, isolating them in a private world of their own—a world suspended in expectation.

'As I love you, Sally, but in a different way.'

'What is your way, Christopher?'

'As a man. A lover. A husband—if you will have me, Sally.'

'How *can* you love me,' she protested, 'when I'm always accusing you wrongly and outrageously?'

He laughed and pulled her into his arms.

'I don't question *how*—I just know that I do. Even when you're being maddening and provoking and damned infuriating. *I love you*, Sally, do you understand? There are no whys and wherefores about love! I want you, just as you are, with all your faults—'

'Indeed! And have I so many?' she retorted indignantly.

'As many as a porcupine has bristles!'

'Is that so? And what about *you*?'

'You'll discover them all after we're married, my darling—I'm not giving you enough time before that! I'm an impatient man. I can't wait.'

She laughed suddenly and felt herself drawn closer to him. She lifted her face to his and for a long moment their private world became the heart of the universe, exquisite and untouchable.

After a while Christopher said gently: 'It's the end of a tradition, Sally. Do you mind?'

'What tradition?' she asked dreamily.

'That there should always be a Doctor Peterson in Tresanton.'

'What does that matter? There'll be two Doctor Maynards, instead.'

'That,' he said with his lips against her hair, 'sounds good to me. Very good.'

'But I'd like one tradition to remain, Christopher—that Creek House should still be the home of the village doctor.'

278

'I'd like that—but only on *my* terms. I'm not a man to live contentedly in my wife's house, you know.'

Sally grinned wickedly.

'I'll sell it to you—gladly. It's mortgaged up to the hilt!'

'In that case I'll sell my own house immediately. I'll see the agents tomorrow. But why are we wasting time discussing details which can very well keep? I've more urgent business to attend to . . .'

'And what is that?'

'Tilt your chin up, woman. I want to kiss you again!'

We hope you have enjoyed this Large Print book. Other Chivers Press or Thorndike Press Large Print books are available at your library or directly from the publishers.

For more information about current and forthcoming titles, please call or write, without obligation, to:

Chivers Press Limited
Windsor Bridge Road
Bath BA2 3AX
England
Tel. (01225) 335336

OR

G.K. Hall & Co.
295 Kennedy Memorial Drive
Waterville
Maine 04901
USA

All our Large Print titles are designed for easy reading, and all our books are made to last.